GHOSTS OF THE PAST

WASTELAND MARSHALS #3

GAIL Z. MARTIN
LARRY N. MARTIN

Cover Design by Robyne Pomroy

This book is a work of fiction. Any resemblance to any person, living or dead, is coincidental. Except that bit about that guy. That's totally a thing.

1

"Go long!" Lucas sent a battered red Frisbee flying. The huge wolf bounded after it, all legs and power, then leaped into the air and snatched the plastic disk with his teeth. He padded back to Lucas, managing an expression of sheepish triumph.

"Let me guess. You put a fang through it—again," Lucas said. The wolf cocked his head in acknowledgment and held up one paw, asking for a treat.

"Go easy on these. We still don't know how they'll affect your other half," Lucas replied as he pulled two dog biscuits from his pocket. He gave one to the wolf, who gobbled it down with a disconcerting crunch, and decided to try one for himself.

"Huh. Not half bad—although a little stale. But what isn't?" he added with a sigh.

The wolf trotted away into a small cluster of trees at the edge of the mountain meadow to shift in privacy, and minutes later, a tall blond man strode out. Shane caught up with Lucas and looked remorsefully at the damaged Frisbee.

"Sorry. Quentin gets really into the game."

"You need to have a talk with your wolf, or we're going to run out of Frisbees," Lucas told him, still adjusting to Shane naming his furry half Quentin. "He's chewed up three already, and it's not like we can just buy one at the store."

Lucas Maddox and Shane Collins grew up together in Cleveland, served in the Army, and then became US Marshals. They had survived battlefields and attempted Mob hits. But nothing had prepared them to survive the cluster-fuck of catastrophes that now, almost four years later, people just called the "Events."

Terrorists had turned the major nations' own nuclear warheads against them, wiping out governments, destroying the financial markets, and devastating the big cities. Millions died from the blast and the radiation. A domino effect of disasters followed—tsunamis, earthquakes, volcanos—killing even more. Then came famine and disease. The power grid largely failed, and any communication systems that remained were spotty and fragile at best.

Law enforcement and the military did their best—those who weren't casualties in the first wave of attacks—but the sheer magnitude of the problems winnowed their numbers. Now what remained were largely local sheriffs, park rangers, and a few others, like Shane and Lucas, who were the last two US Marshals in their three-state area.

"You know, up here in the mountains it's easy to pretend everything didn't crash and burn," Shane mused, looking out over the valley and forest.

"Not hard to remember as soon as we take the horses back on the road."

Shane grimaced. "Yeah. Okay. But sometimes it's nice to just have a flash, a few seconds, where the world isn't fucked and you can almost believe it never happened."

Lucas could hear the sadness in his partner's voice. They had worked closely together for so long, under crazy and dangerous conditions, that they didn't need a lot of words to explain themselves. Even less so now that Lucas had an ancient elemental spirit riding shotgun to keep him alive, and Shane had been turned by a wolf shifter, which heightened his ability to hear the songs of the ancient spirits and enhanced his occasional psychic visions.

"I try not to do that," Lucas admitted, walking over to stand beside Shane, taking in the view. "Just rips the scab open again when you remember how it is now."

"I guess so." Shane sighed. "At least the folks who lived out here had time to come up with a plan. The places we rode past on the way didn't seem to have been abandoned very long. I'm sort of surprised many were empty at all. Figured this would be where folks might fall back to make their stand."

Lucas looked out over the vast forest and the deep clefts and valleys—what people in these parts called "hollows." "I imagine there are some folks holed up for the duration. Hell, some folks in these parts didn't come out even before the Events. They aren't our problem."

Two US Marshals couldn't be everywhere, and they certainly couldn't fully enforce the law or keep the peace—even though Shane and Lucas were no longer fully human, and Lucas would argue, at least on bad days, that they weren't completely sane either. So they did what they could and tried to take care of the problems the locals couldn't. Calling for backup was a lot harder than it used to be, but when Shane and Lucas were needed, desperate people found a way.

Despite the fact that the world had damn near ended, on days like this, Lucas knew how lucky he was to still have Shane riding with him and to still have a purpose for living. Outwardly, not much had changed, except for gaining a few scars along the way.

Shane still had that blond, blue-eyed, All-American cowboy aw-shucks charm that always made witnesses relax and waitstaff flirt. Lucas's dark hair and dark eyes gave off a moody, bad-boy vibe that made playing good cop/bad cop easy. They were almost the same height—nearly six-foot-two inches—but whether or not the heights were an exact match had been a joking point of contention since they'd hit their final growth spurt back in the day.

"You know what I'd like to do, when we're done with this case?" Shane asked. Helping a bunch of scholars protect an archive against a supernatural threat wasn't the strangest request they had gotten.

"I'm afraid to ask. Does Quentin want to find a dog park?" Lucas teased.

Shane gave an exaggerated sniff of disdain. "As if. He thanks you to remember he's a wolf, not a dog."

"Still a canine. Potato, po-tah-to."

Shane rolled his eyes. "If you still had a car, he'd pee on your tires."

"Nice. Classy."

"Anyhow, you know what we haven't done for a while? Find a bar that isn't too wrecked and play some pool," Shane said. "Throw a few darts, just…relax a little, like old times."

"And you'll rope me in for karaoke," Lucas said with an exaggerated sigh. "At least there won't be anyone else to hear us." Or any music to sing along with, but they had long ago learned to make do.

"Of course," Shane said with a grin.

"Everything's strictly B-Y-O-B unless we get really lucky," Lucas reminded him. "Although I still have a bottle of the corn whiskey we bought off that farmer in Maryland."

"Not gonna be picky," Shane said. "I mean, what I'd really like is to order a pizza, watch a horror movie marathon, and then play some Warcraft, but…that's not gonna happen."

No, it wasn't, ever again. And even after four years, Lucas felt the loss like a phantom limb.

They headed back to the horses, packing everything they owned into the duffel bags and saddlebags their horses could carry. Lucas figured that if the weather held, they could make it to Ansted in about two days. That meant stopping for the night somewhere, but they usually had their pick of abandoned homes and farms.

Fayette County, West Virginia, hadn't been thickly settled even before the Events. Coal mining and lumber had propped up a hard-scrabble economy dependent on the stubborn will and strong backs of men who worked hard and died young. For those who lived off the grid—or nearly so—before the Events, little had probably changed, except that coming back into society was no longer a choice since society itself was gone.

Shane chuckled, breaking the silence, and Lucas gave him a puzzled look. "What?"

"I think Rocky likes this area," Shane replied. "Can't you hear him singing?" Shane's ability to hear the "songs" of the elemental spirits—otherwise known as daemons or genius loci—had grown stronger since the Events. So had his ability to catch glimpses of the events, both past and future, although the timing and the focus were still beyond his control.

Lucas turned his attention inward, to the daemon, an immortal spirit who had become his co-pilot to save his life when he'd nearly died on one of their cases. He had nick-named the spirit "Rocky" after the name of the park where the entity had been a genius loci—the elemental spirit of a place. Where Shane sensed those spirits as a song, Lucas and Rocky could have a conversation, albeit in Lucas's mind.

"It's pretty out here," Lucas said with a shrug, getting ready to swing back up into his saddle. "What's not to like?"

Shane suddenly cried out and doubled over, landing on his knees, head clutched in his hands. Lucas was beside him in an instant, gun drawn, covering them while his partner was down and vulnerable.

"Shane, talk to me. What are you seeing?" Lucas knew Shane couldn't speak when one of his visions hit, but he felt the need to maintain a connection and let Shane know he wasn't alone. "You're safe. I'm here. Got your back. Gonna be okay. You pick the damnedest times to log into your weird wi-fi."

Lucas knew from experience there was no moving Shane until his clairvoyant revelation ended. All he could do was remain alert for danger and keep his knee pressed against Shane's shoulder in solidarity, grounding him and making sure he knew Lucas was with him.

A moan let him know Shane had started coming back to himself. Shane fell forward onto his hands and knees and retched. He stayed where he was, body trembling, and Lucas knew it was part of Shane coming back to himself, back to the real world.

"I'm going to get you some water. Don't move."

Lucas sprinted to their horses, still keeping an eye out for an ambush. He grabbed a battered stainless-steel water bottle and dug around their provisions for a protein bar that was long past its expiration date. When he returned, Shane had managed to plant himself on his ass, putting a little distance between him and where he'd been sick. Lucas kicked some dirt over the foul-smelling puddle and then brought the food and water over to Shane.

"You okay?" he asked, taking in his partner's pale, sweaty

face. Visions always kicked Shane's ass, no matter how much the other man tried to hide it.

"Yeah," Shane managed, accepting the items gratefully and rinsing his mouth, then washing down the stale bar with a gulp of water. Lucas noted that Shane wasn't shaking so hard, a sign that the worst of the experience was over.

"You ready to ride?"

Shane managed a wan chuckle. "Times like this, I miss the SUV."

Lucas helped him up, relieved when Shane walked on his own back to the horses. Much as he wanted to know what the vision had revealed, Lucas knew that it always took Shane a while to figure out how to put the images into words.

He tried not to look like he was hovering, fussing with his saddlebag until Shane had gotten into his saddle on his own. Moments later, Lucas had mounted up and snapped the reins to head his horse back toward the highway, sparing a worried glance to check on his partner. Shane still looked dazed, but his color had improved, and he sat his horse solidly, so Lucas forced himself to focus on the route, although it was impossible not to worry.

They rode on, but the lighthearted mood had vanished. Both men rode with loaded shotguns across their laps and handguns tucked into their waistbands.

"I saw bits and pieces of a ritual—human sacrifice," Shane said out of the blue after they had ridden for a while. "Pretty sure the victims were drugged. They didn't fight. Some looked like they were unconscious. Lucky for them."

He paused as if trying to work up the nerve to put the horrific vision into words. "You know those slasher flicks we used to watch? The real thing is a lot worse. But that's what it was like. I couldn't see the face of the person doing the ritual. He had a robe with a hood. The rest…it was like some crazy horror movie with the candles and the symbols and a chant."

"Could you tell why he killed them?" Lucas asked, not envying Shane his virtual front-row seat to the killings.

"He said some kind of incantation, and then this black… slime…seemed to come up through the floor and up his body and then into his mouth." He shuddered. "It looked like a cross between motor oil and hot tar, but it was sentient, Lucas. Whatever it was possessed that man."

"Fuck. Like the bad guys weren't bad enough on their own," Lucas replied. "I was okay with living out the real-life version of *Goodfellas*. We never signed on for *The Exorcist*."

"Yeah, well. We didn't volunteer for *The Day After*, but at least it isn't *Dawn of the Dead*," Shane answered. Lucas figured if his partner could make movie metaphors, he was probably going to be as okay as they ever were.

"What do you think it means?" Lucas asked.

"Dunno. Whoever the killer was, he's juiced up and out there, but what he wants or what he can do with that extra mojo, I've got no idea," Shane said.

They rode for a few hours, spending part of the time in silence as Shane recovered from his vision, and the rest playing a trivia game, Lucas's attempt to take Shane's mind off what he had seen. Shane had chosen the category of "science fiction movies" and tossed out true or false questions from memory. Lucas had picked "fantasy novels" for his category. The game kept them occupied, and even more importantly, kept those memories fresh, of the things they had loved and lost in the Events—the games, movies, TV shows, and books that they might never see again.

Lucas's horse, Shadow, came to an abrupt halt. Shane reined in his horse as well. "What's going on?" Shane asked.

"Ghosts," Lucas replied. "Four of them." He looked away

from the spirits only he could see, which stood in the middle of the roadway, and scanned the area around them.

"They want us to go over there," he said, pointing toward a ranch house not far off the road. It looked abandoned, but they had learned the hard way that appearances could be deceiving.

"Do we stop? There are a lot of ghosts."

Lucas had a silent conference with Rocky. "He doesn't sense any beings in or near the house," Lucas reported. "I have the feeling we should go look."

Shane reached for his shotgun. "Then let's see what's going on."

The ghosts vanished from the roadside, only to reappear on the driveway of the house, then on the front porch. Lucas and Shane dismounted and tethered their horses to the fence. Hand signals from their Army days told Shane to stay with the horses and keep watch, while Lucas headed inside.

Lucas approached carefully, making sure he didn't present an easy target. He crouched beneath the large front window and edged up to look inside. He saw no people and no movement. The only sound was the wind in the trees.

He'd learned a long time ago to trust his gut, and doing so had served him well over the years. Now, his stomach had a tight knot, warning of something bad. Not the prickle at the back of his neck that meant imminent danger, but the certainty that something lay ahead he did not want to see.

Lucas tried the front door, and the sinking feeling when it swung open, unlocked, just added to his tension. The furnished, darkened rooms looked as if a family had just stepped out for the day. Except for the smell of mold and mildew, and beneath that, the coppery tang of blood that Lucas knew far too well.

He swallowed hard and did his best not to flinch when the ghosts showed up in the entrance to the kitchen.

Shotgun raised, he made sure the living room was empty before he walked into the kitchen—and nearly lost his lunch.

Four bodies lay on the blood-soaked floor and sprawled across the table. From the smell and condition, Lucas figured they had been dead for a couple of days. Flies buzzed above the corpses of two men and two women, early to mid-thirties, who had been gutted from sternum to pelvis. Without getting any closer, Lucas tried to make out anything distinctive about their clothing, but it was too blood-soaked for him to make out details.

The burned-down stubs of four pillar candles remained on the corners of the table, where the fourth body lay like an offering. Even with the potent smell of blood, Lucas picked up the stink of ash and sulfur. Strange symbols had been scrawled onto the cabinets and windows in what appeared to be blood.

Holy shit, this is the ritual Shane saw in his vision. Lucas had viewed crime scene photos from ritual murders for some of their cases with the US Marshals. But back then, those rituals hadn't been the real thing. Given the ramp-up of everything supernatural since the Events, Lucas didn't doubt that whatever these people had been sacrificed to achieve was part of real, potent magic. And whatever the ritual had summoned wasn't good.

Lucas looked back to the ghosts, who stood in the hallway. They were dressed differently from their corpses, all of them wearing long gray robes. *A religious cult? Wouldn't be the first we've run into. Although human sacrifice is a new angle.*

"You wanted a witness to your deaths?" he asked, glad to step away from the gory scene. "I see you. I am sorry that you were killed. Will that acknowledgment let you move on?"

Lucas's ability to see ghosts had saved his ass many times when spirits had warned of danger. Now, he wasn't sure what these unlucky revenants wanted from him.

One of the ghosts raised her arms, fists clenched, then crossed them at the wrists. The others did the same.

"You want us to find the people who did this to you?" Lucas guessed, thinking that the pose looked like someone bound with handcuffs.

The ghosts nodded, and Lucas's heart sank.

"You were terribly wronged. But I have no idea how to find your killers," he explained. Being the last two US Marshals in their territory usually gave Lucas purpose, a reason to go on. At other times, like now, the enormity of the task threatened to overwhelm him.

The ghosts repeated the gesture, this time in unison, again and again. The silent "chant" made the message clear. *Find them. Stop them. Make them pay.*

"I can't promise," Lucas said. "There's a lot of territory out there, and I don't have much to go on. But...if I can, I will."

The ghosts nodded solemnly, accepting his offer. One by one, they vanished.

"Lucas? Everything okay in there?" Shane called through the open front door.

Definitely not okay. Lucas swallowed down bile and headed back to where his partner waited.

"That ritual you saw in your vision? Pretty sure it happened right here."

Shane listened as Lucas recounted what had happened, then Lucas kept watch while Shane ducked inside for a corroborating look at the crime scene. He emerged, pale and a little green around the gills.

"Fuck. I know I've seen some of those symbols, but I don't remember the meaning," Shane said.

"Whoever killed those people is out here somewhere—and we've got no idea what they conjured up," Lucas replied.

"Do we need to do something about the ghosts?"

Lucas shrugged. "I can't sense anything keeping them

here, except that they wanted someone to know what happened to them—and they want justice. They'll probably move on when they're ready."

"So I guess we keep our eyes open and watch our backs—same as always," Shane replied.

Knowing that a crazy cultist killer was on the loose made Lucas even less happy about needing to find a place to stop for the night, but they were still too far away from Ansted to finish the trip tonight. They found a solid cement block building with garage bay doors leading to an empty storage room in the back, making it easy to stable the horses. After they let the horses graze and found water for them in a nearby stream, Lucas and Shane brought their mounts in and hunkered down for the night.

"Do you think that ritual—the murders—is connected to the case?" Shane asked as he and Lucas finished a dinner of dried meat, cheese, apples, and bread, washed down with a little whiskey.

"No idea," Lucas replied. "I hope not. But I guess anything's possible." He sighed and leaned back against what had been the service counter. "There's a lot of forest out here—and very few people. Bunch of crazy cultists could go anywhere."

"I hope you're right," Shane replied. "But our luck hasn't been that good lately." He stood and stretched. "Get some sleep. I'll take first watch."

To Lucas's relief, the night passed without incident. They headed out early the next morning, opting to eat a breakfast of bread and cheese on the road.

"We need to find some more coffee somewhere," Shane said. "I'd kill for a latte right about now."

Since the Events, coffee—when they could find it in an abandoned house or not-completely-looted store—was boiled over a campfire. Still, it remained a precious luxury, one Lucas would never take for granted again.

"I'll put it on the top of my list of things to look for," Lucas assured him.

By the time they stopped for lunch and to give the horses a rest, they were only within a few hours' ride of their destination.

"The song isn't right." Shane stared at the blue-green valley like he could force it to give up its secrets. "Can't you feel it? What does Rocky say?"

Well? Lucas asked Rocky.

You knew the mountain was troubled. That is why we came here, was it not?

Yes...but details on the kind of trouble would be really useful.

Lucas could almost feel Rocky trying to figure out how to use human speech—which was new to him—to describe what he sensed.

The energy of the mountain is warped, but it is not poisoned, Rocky replied finally. *It is unusual, but that is how it has been for time beyond memory. Although, stronger now, more...unstable.*

Keep an eye on it, okay?

Your eyes are the only ones I have.

Lucas sometimes forgot that Rocky could be very literal. *I mean, pay attention to the strange energy and let me know if something changes.*

Ah. Of course.

Lucas turned back to Shane. "From what Rocky's picking up, he doesn't think anyone has altered the energy. It's always been that way."

Shane nodded. "That makes sense. Maybe some people could pick up on those vibes. Something has drawn seekers here for centuries. Take that hotel the coven in Bedford asked us to investigate, for example. The Spiritualists who built the Mountain Cove Hotel wanted to find a way to reach across the Veil and contact the dead."

"Except it sounds like the dead started reaching back."

"Yeah, that tends to be a problem."

"The coven really wanted us to come up here," Lucas mused. "Someone must have really put up the Bat-Signal like it was a big deal. I mean, we owe the coven some favors, but helping a bunch of scholar-monks safeguard recorded knowledge in an old hotel that phases in and out of time isn't our usual gig."

"Except nothing's been our usual gig in a long time," Shane replied. "If that ritual I saw in my vision—and the murder house—is somehow related, that's a lot closer to being our kind of thing."

"Those bodies hadn't been there long," Lucas countered. "The coven asked us to swing through here months ago."

"They're witches. Maybe they got a glimpse of the future. Or maybe there's something bigger connecting everything we don't know yet."

"Aren't you a ray of sunshine," Lucas muttered.

"For all we know, things could have blown over a long time ago," Shane said.

"We should be so lucky," Lucas replied. "Because then, we'd probably need to go looking for the killer from your vision."

Shane looked away, and Lucas recognized the guilt that ghosted across his expression. "We could have gotten here sooner. I cost us time."

"You just got turned into a fuckin' werewolf," Lucas countered. "You needed a chance to figure out how all that worked. We both needed to wrap our heads around it."

"Still—"

"You gave me space to process when Rocky first came onboard. Just returning the favor."

They walked back to their horses. Shane patted his roan gelding, named Red. Lucas's black stallion—not-so-creatively named Shadow—bent his head to have his ears scratched.

"Want to do a drive-by to take a look at the old hotel before we go into town looking for the scholars?" Shane asked as he swung up into the saddle. "Since the hotel is at the heart of what the witches wanted us to protect."

"More of a 'ride past,' don't you think?" Lucas snickered, mounting his horse. "Sure. Maybe Quentin or Rocky will pick up on something even if we don't."

At first, it had felt odd to refer to Shane's wolf and Lucas's elemental spirit by different names. After all, it had only been a few months for Lucas, and even less for Shane, and the situations took a lot of getting used to. But as they settled into what was now the "new normal," naming the creatures made conversation clearer and no longer seemed as strange.

They took the exit closest to their destination, and their horses' hoofbeats seemed loud in the otherwise silent, deserted interchange.

"Lucas—look! It's that place we watched the show about on the Haunted History Channel," Shane said, pointing at a garish, faded billboard. Shane's excited tone and big grin made Lucas smile. Leave it to his geeky partner to find another roadside attraction to check out—even after the end of the world.

"You made me watch so many of those shows, it's hard to keep them straight," Lucas teased, although he thought he remembered the episode. Shane had a definite weak spot for quirky tourist traps. It made sense now that they understood Shane's ability to hear the daemon song and that those attractions tended to be built where someone sensed the unusual energy of a genius loci. Those sort of spots tended to either get a sideshow or a shrine.

The Mysterium and Oddity Museum sat just past the off-ramp, where Route 60 connected to Route 19. Lucas spotted the rusted hulk of an old Ferris wheel a mile away.

"I figure you're going to want to stop and poke around?" Lucas asked, but he didn't mind, and Shane knew it.

"Of course! Maybe there'll be a tie-in to the legend of the vanishing hotel," Shane replied.

Lucas reined in his horse, taking in a stockade fence that looked relatively new, running all the way around the main buildings. A sign for the attraction hung on the fence.

"Be careful—I'm not sure it's deserted," Lucas warned. "I'd rather not get a load of buckshot in my pants from an angry owner."

"Why would anyone stick around? I'm pretty sure the tourist trade isn't what it used to be," Shane answered.

"Just sayin'—keep your wits about you," Lucas replied. "That fence doesn't look old enough to have been up before the Events."

"Anything from Rocky? Quentin isn't terribly worried, but he'd like a biscuit."

Quentin wasn't a possessing entity the way Rocky was, but Lucas knew Shane was learning how to "access" that new side of himself even when he was in human form.

Lucas chuckled. "I can get some for both of you, once we get where we're going. Rocky isn't picking up danger. Magic, yes—fairly strong. Possibly protective wardings. And energy deep down. Not another daemon. But maybe ley lines. That's not a term he'd use...but the idea matches."

"Can you pick up anything about ghosts?"

Lucas concentrated. "The old part of the park is definitely haunted."

"I'm not surprised," Shane said as he swung down from

his horse and tethered it to a post at the edge of the parking lot. "I watched this episode a bunch of times—in that crappy hotel in Des Moines with the money-laundering witness."

Lucas groaned. "That place. Lousy cable, the pillows were terrible, and I think we got food poisoning from the restaurant."

"Yep. That's the place. I think the channel was running its '5 Top Episodes' on a loop, and I was probably too sick to bother changing the channel."

Lucas chuckled. "The only saving grace was that our witness was sicker than we were, so he wasn't going to run away."

They didn't intend to leave their horses unprotected, but Shane ventured closer to the unfenced, overgrown area where the rusted rides hunkered. "The original owner of the place was a real piece of work," he recalled.

"Serial killer?" Lucas didn't quite remember.

"Maybe. The park was already past its heyday when the guy bought it. He skimped on maintenance. People got hurt. At first, he paid them off, but then a couple of kids died, and that got him shut down."

"Shit."

Shane nodded. "Yeah. He'd been running the weird little freak show museum as a side gig, but then he expanded when the park closed and added the Mysterium. The show made it sound like he might have bought some haunted—if not cursed—items for the museum. The Mysterium was mostly a bunch of clever visual tricks, but I think he might have tapped into the energy fluctuations around here."

"Ley lines would explain a lot, especially if there are mineral and ore deposits of the right kind in the right places to amplify the energy," Lucas suggested.

Shane nodded. "The original owner just disappeared one day. No body, no blood. Wallet and car keys untouched.

Nothing missing out of the register. Had a safe in his office that hadn't been tampered with, and there was several thousand bucks in it."

"They ever find him?"

"Nope. Not even when they brought in a psychic," Shane added with a smirk, since the whole idea seemed so ironic in a place like this.

"Got a theory?"

"I think he might have messed with something he didn't know how to control. Summoned an entity, called up a creature, that sort of thing. He was on the brink of bankruptcy and foreclosure, and there were lawsuits from the park deaths that were playing out."

"You don't think he just killed himself."

Shane shook his head. "Nah. He was a win-at-any-cost kind of guy. He'd be more likely to murder someone than to commit suicide."

Lucas stood watch and kept the horses while Shane got a good look at the dilapidated Ferris wheel as well as a Tilt-A-Whirl and Scrambler that showed the decay of years exposed to the elements.

"I know everything is a ruin now, but this place is pretty cool." Shane nearly bounced with excitement.

Lucas gave him an assessing look. "Are you picking up on the energy here? Because you're acting like you've had one too many energy drinks."

"Maybe. Quentin's twitchy."

"Great. A twitchy wolf shifter."

"I want to see if we can get inside," Shane said, heading for the main entrance. Lucas followed with an exaggerated, long-suffering sigh. He didn't really mind. The new reality offered few enough opportunities for entertainment.

"Here, watch the horses. I'll knock," Lucas volunteered.

He pulled out his Marshal's badge, just in case anyone was home.

The door opened to reveal a man who had the well-dressed but somber appearance of a funeral director from the 1920s.

"I'm Lucas Maddox, and this is my partner, Shane Collins. We're US Marshals. We were in the area, and to be honest, we thought your place looked interesting. We're hoping we can get a tour if that's possible."

"I would be happy to give you a special tour. I'm Eddie McCoy, the owner. Please, come with me."

Lucas wasn't sure what to make of the man's odd choice of clothing or his slightly antiquated manner of speech. It seemed unlikely he expected any customers, or that he would keep on wearing a costume so long after the world had shut down.

Eddie led them past the ticket counter and into the Oddity Museum. Large glass cases held all kinds of spooky, weird, and occult objects. Taxidermy animals dressed in clothing and posed in dioramas sat next to carved wooden shamans' masks and a Voudon altar. A mummified two-headed goat shared a shelf with a necklace said to have been owned by Lizzie Borden.

"It's like a Cabinet of Wonders," Shane said, using an old Victorian phrase.

Eddie paused in his narration to glance over his shoulder with an approving expression. "Yes. Exactly. When I purchased the museum, I removed the items that were not real. Those that were truly dangerous—cursed or haunted—I destroyed or moved to a safe location. Over the years, I've added to the collection, from things I picked up here and there along the way, and on occasion, from the estates of other collectors."

I believe he is a witch, and he is tied, somehow, to the energy beneath us, Rocky warned. *He may be able to sense me and Quentin. Be careful.*

Eddie looked the part of a well-to-do man from the Roaring Twenties, a rakish Great Gatsby look that suited his tall, thin frame. His dark hair was cut in a style that matched that period, setting off deep-set, piercing eyes. Whether it was natural magnetism or a facet of his magic that gave him charisma, Lucas didn't know, but he could imagine their host on stage, at home in front of the footlights.

Lucas remained looking at the objects behind the glass. "So everything here is real?"

Eddie raised an eyebrow. "I sense that you are both well-equipped to answer that yourself." He didn't press for an answer and led the way to the next part of the attraction. "Please assure your guardians that I intend you no harm."

Lucas and Shane exchanged a glance but said nothing.

"How real is the Mysterium?" Shane asked as they left behind the gallery of oddities. When they stepped over the threshold into the "mystery spot" portion of the building, Lucas felt a frisson of energy that raised the hairs on the back of his neck.

The first few rooms held optical illusions and cleverly designed tricks that made water appear to run up hill, people seem to defy gravity, and other violations of the laws of physics. But as they moved farther inside, Lucas felt a low thrum of energy that practically vibrated in his bones.

"Something's different here." Lucas's eyes narrowed as he looked around the room.

"This area has been considered to be special—maybe even sacred—for a very long time," Eddie replied. "The ley lines beneath the ground—rivers of natural energies—converge here. Over time, they fluctuate. Where the Mountain Cove Hotel once stood was a powerful confluence for the lines and the telluric energies—called a vortex. And then a shift occurred and created an unusual concentration of energy that became a rift of sorts—an anomaly."

Eddie shook his head. "Put a vortex and an anomaly together, and it's an energy beacon, where the powers converge and don't always work the way they're supposed to."

"So it's natural, but not original," Shane clarified.

"Yes. And since it has shifted before, it could at some point shift again," Eddie replied. "The changes I've made to the grounds and the collections brought the energies here into alignment. Now, this is an anchor."

"Are you part of that anchor?" Shane asked, and Lucas wondered if his partner chose to go on the offensive since it seemed clear Eddie had picked up on their unusual natures.

Eddie inclined his head in acknowledgment. "Yes. I have chosen to link myself to this place to strengthen that protection. I draw my magic from the bones and humours of the earth," Eddie replied. "Stone, minerals, ore, and gems, as well as the caves and rivers. I can touch the ley lines, and the telluric currents, and the magnetism at the core of the world."

"Why become an anchor?" Lucas asked, curious and wary. "The world pretty much ended. I mean, the movie is over, and we're just sweeping up the popcorn before the theater turns out the lights. So why make that kind of commitment now?"

Eddie regarded Lucas with a look that he couldn't quite read. "Then, why not? If there is no other purpose remaining, why not take meaning from what can still be done?"

Lucas opened his mouth to argue, and shut it again, remaining silent.

A hint of a smile touched Eddie's thin lips. "Is that not what you and your partner do every day? Create meaning from purpose, doing what you are still able to do? I think you understand my reasons very well."

"Are you immortal?" Shane asked, surprising Lucas at his boldness.

Eddie chuckled. "I don't know. I haven't died yet. I don't really want to test it, although I suspect I am." He leveled a knowing gaze at them. "As are you."

Lucas shifted, uncomfortable. "Like you said, not something we want to prove the hard way."

"Mountain Cove has long attracted untrained psychics. Now, it draws people whose abilities surfaced or strengthened in the upheaval of natural energies after the Events," Eddie told them. "They came into their powers without teachers, desperate for guidance. Too many mistake the ability to connect with those energies as dominion over them. They are wrong."

"Thank you for the tour," Lucas said, hoping Shane would pick up on the cue that it was time to leave. "We need to be going."

"I'm glad you stopped," Eddie said, and while his welcome felt genuine, Lucas couldn't shake the feeling that Eddie knew something they didn't. "I hope we'll meet again." He paused. "A word of warning—a new camp just sprang up on the way to the hotel. They aren't very friendly. You might want to keep your distance."

Lucas and Shane thanked him again for the tour and then headed up the mountain toward the hotel and the scholars who had requested their help.

"So, what did you think of Eddie?" Lucas asked. Rocky hadn't weighed in with an opinion yet, which was odd.

"Quentin wasn't sure about him," Shane replied. "I liked the grounds and the building. Definitely my kind of place—too bad the gift shop wasn't open," he added with a grin. "I don't understand the old-fashioned clothing."

Lucas shrugged. "I guess he can wear whatever he wants, what with the apocalypse and all. Not like anyone is going to turn him in to Human Resources."

"You didn't ask him about the crazy cultists."

Lucas gave him a look. "Great way to make a good first impression. I'd be like, so...we just met you, but we found mutilated bodies a ways back. You wouldn't happen to know anything about them, would you?"

Shane rolled his eyes. "I guess you've got a point. Maybe we can stop here on the way back. After all, if he's a witch, maybe he can find things out we can't."

"Or, he's in cahoots with whoever did the ritual," Lucas pointed out. "Could go either way."

2

They rode for a while, leaving the interstate highway behind them and following a slightly smaller, winding road toward the hotel.

"I thought everyone had cleared out from these parts except for the scholars," Lucas said as they spotted a sign for the town of Hico, a small settlement that clearly wasn't completely abandoned.

"So did I. Maybe it's that unfriendly camp Eddie warned us about," Shane replied.

Hico appeared to be little more than a few buildings and a couple of houses near a crossroads. It looked to Lucas as if there had been an old-time general store and a gas station long enough ago that the buildings had probably been repurposed. A boxy building might have been a Grange or community hall, and an old church sat nearby, white paint peeling, steeple broken off. Five or six farmhouses sat scattered around the crossroads. None of the buildings looked newer than a hundred years.

Several wagons sat beside a barn. Two men went in and

out of the building, and with the doors open, Lucas could see horses stabled inside.

Rocky felt restless in the back of Lucas's mind as if he didn't like the situation.

Lucas spotted only adults, no children. That told him the group wasn't a family cluster that had sought shelter after the Events. Maybe they were a religious group, he thought, which seemed likely since the people he saw moving from one building to the next wore what looked like monks' cassocks. More than one person stopped to stare as they rode by. No one raised a hand in greeting or called out to them, a bad sign in Lucas's book.

A cold chill ran down Lucas's spine as he realized where he had seen robes like the settlers wore. *Those look like the odd clothing the ghosts wore, back at the murder house.*

Lucas cleared his throat, getting Shane's attention. He dropped one hand to his hip level, somewhere the settlers wouldn't see, and made the hand signal for "trouble." Shane met his gaze and nodded, both of them now on alert.

He and Shane always rode with their weapons loaded and in easy reach, conspicuously displayed to discourage trouble-makers. Lucas wondered if the settlers were merely distrustful of strangers—not unreasonable, given the circum-stances—or if they took the two of them for outlaws. He was long past caring, having found that instilling a little fear by their appearance reduced the number of idiots who tried to start something they had to finish.

"No gardens. Haven't been here very long then," Shane noted under his breath. More permanent settlements needed a reliable food supply, which meant gardens, fruit trees, and livestock like chickens and goats. "From how high the weeds are, and since the tall grass hasn't been trampled down, I'd say they might have just arrived."

"They're a long way from everywhere," Lucas said. Before

the Events, the big draw here had been outdoor adventures—whitewater boating on the New River, hiking in the mountains, zip lines, and rustic cabin rentals. That's what had sustained the restaurants, hotels, and outfitting shops down near the highway exit—all of them long shuttered and abandoned.

"For the record, Quentin doesn't like them. His hackles are up and he's growling."

"Rocky's not too keen on them, either. Just as well we're only passing through." Lucas wondered how many people were part of the ramshackle community. He saw at least a dozen moving between the buildings. Smoke rose from the chimneys of several houses, suggesting more people were inside.

"I wonder what the scholars make of them," Lucas said, as they rode beyond the crossroads and headed toward the site of the old hotel. "They don't strike me as friendly neighbors."

"We'll get the chance to ask when we see them tonight," Shane replied.

They fell silent for a while, both men cautiously glancing over their shoulders to assure that no one from the hamlet had followed them. It didn't appear to Lucas that they had picked up any stalkers, but he couldn't shake the uneasiness he'd felt in Hico.

"For this area having been a kinda big deal at one time, there's not much left," Shane observed as the sound of their hoofbeats echoed on the empty road.

From the rusted sign for Osborne Creek and the few natural landmarks, Lucas knew they were close to the old Spiritualist community's location, with the mysterious hotel that might or might not still be there.

The witches had told them about the area, back when they had asked for the two men's help. Mountain Cove had been founded back in 1851 by two spirit mediums who led a pilgrimage down from New York to claim land near Osborne Creek in what was at that point still a part of Virginia. Their community started out well, building homes, a school, a mill, and stores, as well as a newspaper and the hotel, before fizzling out just a few years later.

"It's just spooky that people built all those buildings and there's nothing left except the hotel—which is apparently only here sometimes," Lucas replied.

Shane shrugged. "I imagine if we went snuffling through the underbrush, we'd find stone foundations, old wells, maybe a millstone or two." Shane scanned for danger as he got the lay of the land.

"Snuffling?" Lucas joked. "Gonna pick up a few truffles while we're rooting around?"

"It's as good a word as any," Shane defended with a grin. "But back to your point—the community was here and gone ten years before the Civil War. There were battles fought all around these parts. An awful lot of buildings didn't survive being in the path of two armies."

"But the hotel hung on until about 1920," Lucas said. "At least, that's what was in the information the scholars sent us. And then it got weird."

"It's been a long time since things weren't weird." Shane snorted.

A lot has happened since the 1850s, Lucas thought, as he tried to picture the area as it must have looked when the religious community put down roots. This stretch of road had flat areas off to each side or gradually sloping hills. Both were at a premium in notoriously hilly West Virginia. In his mind's eye, Lucas could imagine wooden storefronts, modest homes, and on Osborne Creek—which they had just crossed over on a bridge—a mill. If he paid close attention, he could make out where older trees began and younger ones left off

—an indication that the land with the new growth had once been something else.

Still, Lucas had visited a lot of abandoned areas—both from before the Events and even more modern ruins from afterward. Few had been as completely obliterated as the village of Mountain Cove.

Shane came to an abrupt stop, and a look of pain lanced across his face.

Lucas, stop!

Lucas heard Rocky's voice in his mind, and he pulled up on the reins.

The energy here is powerful, but...damaged. Be very careful.

"Did you feel it?" Lucas and Shane asked in unison.

"We have to be close to where the hotel was," Shane said with a grimace that told Lucas the discomfort hadn't eased. "I got a killer headache out of nowhere, and the song in my mind is really fucked up."

"Rocky just yelled for me to stop," Lucas replied, although he felt twitchy, skin prickling, hair rising at the back of his neck, and a pervasive sense of *wrongness* telling his hindbrain to run. "What do you mean, the song is fucked up?"

Shane turned his horse around and rode back a few yards. Lucas backtracked to join him. The twitchiness Lucas felt eased but didn't completely disappear.

"When the genius loci of a place is 'happy,' for lack of a better term, the song is calm. Not necessarily something you can start humming along to, but peaceful in a natural sort of way," Shane explained. "And when there's dark magic or something really terrible left a stain on the land, it's more like a horror movie soundtrack—discordant and creepy." He shook his head. "The song just ahead sounds like a hundred different marching bands and orchestras all playing different pieces of music—all different styles—at the same time."

Lucas nodded. "I don't hear the song, but I definitely got

the gut reaction to 'get the hell out of Dodge.' Let me see if Rocky can explain it any better."

He closed his eyes, concentrating as he thought the question at his co-pilot.

The energy of the area right in front of you is...folded in on itself. Layered. Like it is in many places at once, but also all here, Rocky replied.

What does that even mean? How can energy have layers? Lucas thought for a moment. *People say the hotel fades in and out. Do you mean that it's here—and not here—at the same time?*

That is how it feels, reading the energy.

Lucas opened his eyes and blinked. "I think we've got Schrödinger's hotel. It's there—and it's not there. But its energy is all piled up."

"Like a double exposure? The way people could take photographic film and layer it to make it look like there were images on top of images, back before computers," Shane replied. "The end result looked real, but it was actually a composite, made up of all the pieces."

"I guess?" Lucas felt completely out of his element. "Even Rocky didn't seem to have run into this before."

Shane chewed on his lip as he thought. "The Spiritualists built the hotel expecting that people would come to visit their community seeking answers, or maybe come to learn about their beliefs. Most of the people who moved here believed they had some level of psychic gift, and the two founders were supposedly strong mediums. Maybe there were enough people with abilities that they somehow...I don't know, *bent* the energy?"

"Then why didn't that happen in Salem, Massachusetts, with all the witches, or New Orleans, with the Voodoo?" Lucas argued. "Why out here in the middle of West fuckin' Virginia?"

Shane shrugged. "No clue. Maybe the original spirit of the

land was already wobbly, and all that extra energy knocked it off its axis."

"Well, we're either going to have to ride past where the hotel was, or go a whole hell of a long way around, because there aren't a lot of side roads in this forest," Lucas replied. "Not to mention, backtrack through that creepy little town."

"The scholars are holed up in the Ansted library," Shane said. "It's about four miles down the road. On the other side of a whole bunch of cemeteries, once we get past the freaky hotel."

"This just keeps getting better," Lucas muttered. "Let's lead the horses through the bad part and hope it eases up pretty quickly."

Red and Shadow were both good-tempered, and they'd already learned to accept gunfire as well as Shane's wolf. Lucas hoped the horses wouldn't try to bolt. Still, he didn't want to risk being thrown or losing one of their mounts.

Shane and Lucas slipped down from their saddles and offered their horses treats before taking the reins and walking down the empty road.

The prickle on his skin grew worse until Lucas felt like he should be brushing off a legion of spiders. Shadow obediently stayed beside him, but the horse's eyes were wide, and now and again, a tremor passed through the huge, powerful body, although his training held, and he did not try to run.

"Hang in there, boy. Not too much longer," Lucas coaxed, hearing Shane make the same comforting promises to Red.

Lucas tried to calm his horse, contain his own reactions, scan for danger, and get a look at the spot where the cursed hotel must have stood. That was a lot to do all at once. Lucas just wanted to get out of the zone affected by the strange energy.

A glance at his partner told him Shane shared his struggle. Except where Lucas fought off a sense of dread and the lizard-brain urgency to run, Shane's pinched features told Lucas the other man struggled against physical pain.

Rocky—can whatever this is hurt us?

Rocky didn't answer immediately, making Lucas worry that the energy fluctuations could affect even a strong elemental spirit.

It cannot hurt me...and therefore, us. I am less sure about Shane. But it makes thinking difficult. I think your word is...static. Fuzzy noise and blurry picture.

Lucas had to chuckle, wondering how Rocky had fished the idea of TV white noise out of his brain. While there were a few sets still working, and DVD players were precious and rare, Shane and Lucas hadn't seen anything since the broadcast stations went down during the Events. The news reports had winked out, one by one, until nothing remained except a gray buzz.

Then again, maybe it wasn't so hard to figure out after all. Those images regularly haunted Lucas's dreams, and Rocky was along for the ride.

How much farther?

Just past those boulders. We are in the center of the disturbance. If you wished to see where the hotel stood, this is the likely spot, Rocky said.

Lucas pointed to the hillside on their right, and Shane gave a curt nod as if every movement hurt. A large area had been cut into the hillside at its base, and Lucas could imagine the land gradually sloping away behind the three-story clapboard hotel sketched in the notes they had received. It would have looked out over the valley, a panoramic vista.

Now that he took in the contours of the land, both natural and man-made, Lucas knew they had come to the right place. He even glimpsed the crumbling remnants of cement steps rising from the roadway and vanishing into a tangle of brambles.

Shadow fidgeted, letting Lucas know they needed to get moving. He jerked his head to indicate moving forward and picked up his pace.

As soon as they passed the outcropping of large boulders, the troublesome energy vanished as if they had stepped through a curtain.

They put several yards between them and the anomaly, and then Lucas stopped. He leaned forward to rest his forearms on Shadow, trying to regain his bearings. Both he and his horse were breathing hard, muscles trembling, covered with a thin sheen of sweat in testimony to the physical struggle of containing their fear and the uneasiness created near the "missing" hotel.

"There is no way anyone with a whiff of psychic ability could feel comfortable spending the night in a hotel room if the energy always feels like that," Shane said, his voice rough, breath coming in pants as if they had sprinted.

"Dude, I don't think that anyone with a working brain stem would feel comfortable. We've felt some bad mojo in places, but nothing quite so...wrong."

They paused to let the horses graze and took a moment to replenish themselves with water from their wineskin and some dried meat and fruit. Lucas kept staring at the road where they had just been, still worried that they might have attracted unwanted attention from the squatters in Hico.

"Come on," Shane said, pulling him out of his thoughts. "I don't want to be out here when it gets dark, and we're going to lose the light before too long. We still don't know where we're staying when we get to Ansted."

What went unspoken was the reminder that the map showed several cemeteries between here and their destination. Old, untended cemeteries next to a volatile well of psychic energy. *Yeah, that can't be good.*

Now that they were past the site of the old hotel, Lucas

and Shane saddled up and rode for Ansted. Lucas felt hyper-vigilant, so attuned to sound and movement that he might jump out of his skin. One look at Shane told him that his partner had picked up on the same wariness.

"You getting anything different with the song of the place?" Lucas asked, needing to break the silence.

Shane looked like he was struggling to put his thoughts into words. "There are a number of different genius loci in this area, which isn't that unusual in a place like this. It's always remained fairly wild, and part of it was a park. The elemental spirits weren't drowned out in the noise of development. This section has a much more peaceful song than the section near the old hotel site."

"Quentin picking up anything?"

Lucas knew that Shane still had a lot to learn about his new wolf nature. He'd been bitten by a hybrid shifter, a weaponized creature created by a secret government project. So while he could shift without being driven by the moon cycle, the senses of an apex predator always lurked just below the surface of his mind.

"He's jumpy as fuck. Keeps growling. It's giving me a headache."

Before he had Rocky's consciousness in his mind, Lucas might have ribbed his partner about referring to his wolf as a separate person. Now, Lucas understood completely what it was like to have another entity riding shotgun in his noggin.

"Is he getting any kind of sense from the surroundings? Any critters out there we need to be watching for—supernatural or not?" This area had always been remote. Bear, bobcats, and wolves survived in the less-settled areas, even before the world fell apart. Since then, Lucas and Shane had seen the creatures' numbers multiply in the forests where the two marshals had traveled.

Most people left rural areas when the power grid failed,

and when enough pieces of society fell apart that supply shipments no longer came, stores closed down. Now that the people were gone, the animals had taken back the mountains —and even some of the cities.

"There's something trailing us. Quentin thinks it's human —but not a 'regular' person. Maybe someone with magic, or psychic ability?" Shane replied.

He pinched the bridge of his nose, a sure sign that his head still ached. "Between the vibe you give off with Rocky and the sense most animals seem to pick up from Quentin, I don't think the regular wildlife are going to cause a problem."

"How far back is our stalker?" Lucas asked, automatically looking around.

"Not sure."

"Someone from Hico? You think they're actually stalking us, or just going in the same general direction?"

Shane shrugged. "No way to know. I guess we wait and see."

Lucas felt Rocky flinch as they rode closer to a long flat area tucked into a cleft in the steep hills. Weeds choked the clearing, and trees had begun to reclaim the open land. Lucas felt a chill and guessed they had found one of the cemeteries.

The old burying ground had been abandoned long before people left because of the Events. The town of Ansted had hung on as jobs vanished and young people deserted to find new horizons. Like many of the little villages in these hills, it had faced a bleak future with an aging population and no real prospects. Then the world burned, and hanging on wasn't enough.

Lucas thought he glimpsed weathered headstones amid the tall grass, stained granite too worn by time to be readable. He could almost guess the age of the headstones from their shape, and he wondered if the long-ago Spiritualists who staked out their brief, doomed community had left any of their faithful behind.

Did a village of spirit mediums and psychics mind having several old cemeteries right on their border? Or did people choose to bury their dead here because they sensed the fluctuating energy, even before it grew stronger?

I am not sure the dead here rest in peace, Rocky observed, although Lucas had not asked. *I sense restless spirits, some disturbed enough to be a danger. The strange energy may have kept some of them from moving on.*

Trapped them? Or merely confused them so they couldn't find the way out? Lucas asked.

I do not know. But they remain.

Even before his alliance with Rocky, Lucas had an ability to see and talk to ghosts. That talent had grown stronger since the cataclysm, just like Shane's visions and his ability to hear the "songs" of the genius loci had strengthened. Lucas tuned in to his ghost-sense as they rode past the graveyard, alert for trouble.

The temperature dipped, enough to notice, too much to be due to a bit of shade from the trees or clouds blocking the sun. That confirmed Rocky's report, even if the spirits chose not to show themselves to Lucas or lacked the ability to make themselves seen. For now, at least, Lucas left the ghosts alone. Later, he might need to ask them questions, but he did not want to bother them more than once.

Shadow whinnied softly, and Lucas patted his neck. Horses could sense spirits, and while neither of their mounts panicked when Lucas's talent manifested ghosts, he didn't want to push his luck, especially not here.

The day warmed when they passed the first cemetery and dipped again as they rode past the second one. This graveyard was newer, closer to town, and the ghosts had not faded quite so much. They hung back, aware but invisible, watching, taking the measure of two strangers riding into an abandoned town. Lucas felt the weight of their appraising gaze and squared his shoulders, raising his head.

I'm not here to cause you trouble. But if you start it, we'll finish it, he warned silently.

The second cemetery didn't resonate as strongly. Maybe being newer, it hadn't had as long exposure to the volatile energy of the old hotel. Perhaps since it was farther away, the odd fluctuations affected its spirits less, allowing them to rest quietly. Whatever the reason, neither Lucas nor Shane had a reaction as they passed by.

The town of Ansted had seen boom and bust. Remembering what the coven had told them, Lucas knew that when the Spiritualists came, first in the 1830s and then in the 1850s, they named the town New Haven. After the Spiritualists were gone, the stagecoaches came, making the town an important depot. When the railroads took over, a main rail line ran nearby, and the town grew. Coal, iron, and lumber brought wealth and a new name, Ansted, after one of the coal barons. In time, those industries faded, and the town managed to survive, mostly due to its proximity to good hiking and rafting, and Civil War battlefields. Then the Events happened, and people had no reason to stay.

"You'd think after everything, ghost towns wouldn't seem so creepy," Lucas said as they rode into the abandoned downtown. Four years of hard storms and neglect had taken a toll with broken windows, damaged roofs, and toppled signs. The older, more solidly built homes had endured reasonably well, but faded paint and downed trim made it clear no one was home.

"That's because they look normal—but they aren't," Shane observed. "Think about it. If you could see where a blast leveled buildings and burned half the town, you wouldn't wonder where the people went. But that isn't what happened out here. It looks like people just up and left—because they did."

"Yeah. Creepy."

Rocky remained silent, which meant he hadn't sensed danger. Shane hadn't commented, so that meant he and Quentin hadn't learned anything more about whatever had been following them, either.

Towns like Ansted felt melancholy to Lucas. From the shuttered stores and restaurants to the slowly decaying homes, schools, and public buildings, the emptiness was just one more reminder that the way things were before the Events would never be again.

"There's the library." Shane pointed to a granite building solid enough to have been a fallout shelter, back in the day. Lucas wagered that the bars over the windows were a new addition, but otherwise, the library looked unscathed.

If anyone still remained in Ansted aside from the scholars they had come to see, those people weren't making themselves visible. That suited Lucas just fine.

"Well, let's go see what all the fuss is about." Lucas tethered his horse to a tree outside the library and so did Shane. Then they approached the library's big front doors warily, badges in hand.

The doors open, and a middle-aged, balding, and bespectacled man greeted them. Lucas thought he had the look of an academic. Lucas gave his usual introduction. "The coven in Bedford asked us to stop by when we were in the area," he added. "Sorry it's taken us a while, but there's a whole lot going on, and only two of us." He didn't feel compelled to explain that they had taken some time to recover and come to terms with his partner becoming a wolf.

"Marshals. Thank you for coming. You've actually arrived at a good time." The man who welcomed them reminded

Lucas of his high school biology teacher. "I'm Bill Royston. Please, follow me. You must be tired from your journey."

"Is there a way we can get water for our horses?" Shane asked. "We let them graze a while back, but we weren't close to a stream."

"I'll send someone out to give them water. And we converted a building next door to be a stable, so they'll have shelter for the night," Royston told them. "Of course, we can accommodate you here. You'll be safe and reasonably comfortable. The food's pretty good too, considering everything," he added with a conspiratorial wink.

"The coven said something about wanting to preserve knowledge for future generations—in a hotel that isn't always present?" Lucas continued as they followed Royston farther into the building.

"You cover a huge territory, and there must be many places that need you. We wouldn't have imposed except we have a rather unusual situation," Royston replied.

"Why don't you fill us in?" Shane said, as their host brought them to the staff break room. They sat down at the table, and Royston set out a plate of homemade cookies.

"We've been fortunate that the towns near here still had a lot of supplies," the man told them. "And we have access to plenty of cookbooks," he added with a wry smile. "Supplies don't last forever, so we figured—cook it if you've got it."

"I will never pass up cookies," Lucas said and reached for two. Shane helped himself as well, and Royston brought them glasses of tea, then joined them at the table.

"Before things fell apart, I taught at the community college," the man said. "When ...it...happened, before things here got too bad, my colleagues and I realized that knowledge would be one of the most valuable things lost if we didn't act fast."

Lucas could see the weight of the last years in the man's

posture and his worried expression. "We've seen many universities that became armed fortress communities, guarding their libraries, maintaining their node on the internet, and protecting people who have the skills to help us rebuild."

Royston nodded. "We've gotten word that they tried to do that up in Morgantown, at the university. But then the nuclear plants..."

He didn't need to finish the statement. Lucas and Shane knew. Between the earthquakes and tornadoes, many plants sustained serious damage, more than could be fixed by the remaining skeleton crews and their stockpiled parts. The lucky ones were able to shut down before they melted down or leaked radiation. The plant near Morgantown hadn't been lucky.

"The university is still there, of course, but too dangerous to access—for the foreseeable future," Royston continued. "Our beautiful state has been taken advantage of for centuries, resources carted away, and damage not put right. Now, with the earthquakes and the wild storms, that is all coming back to haunt us."

"What do you mean?" Shane asked.

"These hills are riddled with tunnels, left behind from the shaft mines. It's not uncommon for sinkholes to open up. Some are only a few feet across. Others swallow whole towns," Royston replied. "Timber harvesting and strip mines make the slopes dangerous for landslides. The water in many places hasn't been safe without purification for a long time with all the mine runoff. Not to mention the power plants and nuclear sites. What that all adds up to is, there's nowhere that's truly safe to fortify an archive."

"So what's your alternative?" Lucas asked.

"We have been acquiring all of the books, microfiche, and digital resources we can scavenge," Royston answered. "We enlisted all of our colleagues who were willing and able to help. For a while, they brought us materials by the truckload. Eventually, that slowed to a trickle. We don't claim to have everything. But we have a lot. And with the big museums and archives in Washington DC and New York City destroyed... well, we believe it's important to save as much as we can."

Shane looked pained at the recap and Lucas understood. Both of them liked to read and had passed the long hours while on stakeouts or protecting witnesses with books. Since the Events, they carried a few treasured favorites with them and checked deserted homes, stores, and libraries whenever the opportunity presented itself to pick up anything they could.

"So you're the modern version of the Library of Alexandria?" Lucas asked.

Royston chuckled. "Well, we're trying to be the version that doesn't burn. Once we realized that nowhere in West Virginia was truly safe for long-term storage, we saw the potential of Mountain Cove Hotel."

Lucas raised an eyebrow. "You want to move the materials into a place that doesn't exist?"

Royston met his gaze, dead serious. "Oh, it exists. Sometimes. The building phases in and out. We observed and charted the pattern. That was six months ago. We've been moving materials in as fast as we can, given our limited number of people and the fluctuations of the hotel. We've glimpsed a couple of ghosts—and a guy named Fenton at the front desk who seems pretty solid for a spirit."

"So the hotel is real? It's not some kind of ghost?" Shane asked.

"I think it would be accurate to say it's both, because of the unusual energy of the location. Which leads to the reason we asked for your help."

He drained his glass of tea and licked his lips nervously.

"We aren't the only ones who have noticed the energy anomaly of the old hotel. This area has always attracted people with psychic gifts, as far back as there have been Westerners in these parts, and before that, among the tribes. Some people say it calls to them. Others can sense its energy and come to use it for their own purposes."

"We thought we might have been followed, but didn't see anyone," Lucas said.

"It wouldn't be the first time the hotel's drawn the wrong kind of attention," Royston said. "Seems to be happening more and more now that people aren't in shock anymore over the Events. We've had folks show up to try to break into the hotel, or worship it, or exorcise it. Between Mama Jean, Doc, and Eddie, we've been able to send them away—mostly peacefully."

"Eddie? Eddie McCoy, the guy with the Mysterium?" Lucas asked.

Royston nodded. "Yes. He helps to protect us and the hotel."

"And that group we saw in Hico?" Shane asked. He gave a brief recap of what they observed. They had agreed not to mention the murder house until they had a better feel for the scholars and the situation.

"Probably more troublemakers," Royston replied. "I'll let the others know. Mama Jean can put down some extra wardings."

"I'm still not sure why you requested us," Lucas said. "Two Marshals, even with weapons, aren't much of a security detail."

Royston looked up, surprised. "Your skills will enable you to heal the hotel so it's safer for us to move in. There's no one else we know of with those abilities, and I'm afraid that time is running out."

Lucas felt his heart rate spike. *How could they have possibly known about Rocky and Quentin? Hell, when we talked to the coven, it was before Rocky saved my life and before Shane had been bitten.* Then he remembered Eddie's friendliness—and the way he seemed to know just by looking at them about Rocky and Quentin.

Lucas was willing to bet money that Eddie knew exactly who they were when they showed up. *If he was behind the request to bring us here, why pretend like he didn't know us?*

Lucas and Shane looked at each other, confused and wary. "There was nothing in the coven's request about 'abilities' or 'special skills.' We rode a long way to get here. What game are you playing?"

Royston held up his hands in appeasement. "No game, I swear. Sending for you wasn't my idea." He sighed and shook his head. "That's what I get for asking a seer for advice."

Lucas was just about to demand answers when the door opened and a man walked in, dragging a second man by the arm.

"I caught this one lurking outside," the taller newcomer said. "Can't think of any good reason for him to be here—but I sure can come up with a bunch of bad ones."

The prisoner was a man in his late twenties, with an untrimmed beard and long hair pulled back in a queue. He wore the same sort of robe that Lucas had spotted on the newcomers in Hico. His wrists were bound with handcuffs that looked to Lucas like real silver, with sigils carved into the metal that glowed.

"Marshals, this is Doc Swanson. Doc, these are the Marshals that Mama Jean suggested we send for," Royston said, putting a little extra emphasis on the woman's name. "The ones you and Eddie took care of contacting?"

Doc Swanson looked to be in his middle years, bald, with glasses, average height with a slight paunch, wearing khaki pants and a golf shirt. "Pleased to meet you."

"I don't know what's going on here, but we aren't doing one damned thing more until we get some answers," Lucas said, letting his temper show.

"You'll get them," Doc said. "But first, we need to know why this one was sneaking around." Doc shoved the prisoner to sit in the remaining open chair. "Start talking."

The robed stranger just glared at Doc. "You wouldn't understand."

Doc leaned into his space. "Try me. And I want to hear from the demon—not just the poor sap he possessed."

Lucas and Shane traded an alarmed glance. "Demon?" Lucas questioned. "Do you mean daemon?"

The prisoner's eyes glowed red, and he tried to lunge from his chair, but the point of Doc's silver-bladed knife jabbed into his neck, raising a bead of blood.

"Sit down. And start talking."

The stranger sat, but the baleful glare he fixed on Doc promised bloody retribution. Lucas couldn't help remembering the black ooze Shane glimpsed in his vision. *Could that have been a demon?*

"First order of business is to exorcise him and get rid of the son of a bitch that's possessing him," Doc said.

"You can't," the prisoner taunted, his mouth curling into a sneer. He shifted so that the sleeve of his robe rode up on his forearm, exposing a recent, barely healed burn in the shape of a complex symbol. "That brand locks me in this body. Can't throw me out. The only way to get rid of me is to kill him."

Royston got up and called down the hall to someone, but Lucas was too focused on the prisoner to hear what was said.

Doc's face took on a distant expression, one that made Lucas think of how he felt when he spoke to Rocky or contacted ghosts. No sooner had Lucas thought of spirits than he saw one take shape right behind the prisoner, the ghost of a woman Lucas recognized as a victim from the murder house. Lucas startled. That was enough for Doc to give him the once-over as if he knew what Lucas saw.

"If you won't talk, the ghost who's with you can probably tell me everything I need to know," Doc said as if interrogating a spirit was no big deal.

"Have it your way," the demon said with a shrug.

The prisoner's entire manner shifted abruptly. He looked up at Doc. "Please, you've got to help me. Kill me. Stop the torment." His voice sounded like he'd been gargling broken glass—or screaming for hours.

With the demon at the fore, he'd looked healthy, if a bit too skinny. Stripped of that demon glamor, the man looked one step removed from the grave. Sunken eyes, sallow skin, and hollow cheeks made Lucas suspect that the demon fed off the man's energy—and maybe his soul. Lesions covered his skin, raw and oozing. His cracked lips bled. But it was the pain and fear in his haunted eyes that convinced Lucas that death would be a reprieve.

The man glanced up sharply, trying to figure out whether Doc was telling him the truth or not. "Leave her out of it."

Doc was silent for a moment. "She's worried about you. Julie. That's her name. And you're Kenny. You lost her recently. The grief is fresh for both of you. But you think that somehow, there's a way to bring her back? And you're not the only one. Hmm. We need to have a little chat, Kenny."

Kenny had gone pale, eyes wide. "How did you do that?"

Doc spared him a slight twitch of a smile. "You may have a bit of ability to see spirits, but I'm a full psychic medium with a long life of experience. You'd be surprised what I see." At that last sentence, Doc shifted his gaze to meet Lucas's eyes, and Lucas felt sure that the other man read far more about him than Lucas had hoped to reveal.

"I'll tell you anything you want to know. Just please,

promise that you'll kill me. It's the only way I'll ever be free," Kenny begged.

"Julie was murdered. And she wasn't the only one," Doc said. "That's part of how you were possessed. Trading lives for power."

Lucas looked up sharply and so did Shane. *Shit, the murder house is connected. Vengeful ghosts are one thing, but demons? What the fuck did we get ourselves into?*

"Now...tell me about Hayden Montgomery," Doc said. Lucas saw that, like the handcuffs, a line of finely etched runes along the blade blazed. "And I want to talk to Kenny, not the demon possessing him."

"It wasn't supposed to go like this," Kenny said, sounding miserable. "Julie and I went to Hayden's 'Maximize Your Potential' masterclass four years ago. It was at a retreat center in the North Carolina mountains. That's where we were when the Events happened. All of a sudden, none of us could go home."

Sadness colored Kenny's features. "Hayden was wonderful about taking charge. Everyone worked together, and we managed to turn the resort into a self-sustaining commune. What else could we do?"

"You were at a business retreat and ended up demon possessed?" Shane echoed, incredulous.

Kenny shrugged. "More of a self-actualization, motivational intensive small group workshop."

Lucas chuckled. "Wow. I haven't heard that many buzzwords since the bombs hit."

Shane rolled his eyes. Lucas grinned, completely unrepentant. "So what happened next?" Lucas prodded.

"Part of the original event was supposed to be about discovering our hidden psychic abilities," Kenny said. "Mostly like learning to trust your intuition, paying attention to your dreams. So everyone there had an interest in that sort of thing. But after the Events, people started to find that their abilities really were getting stronger."

"It wasn't just you," Shane said. "Same thing seems to have happened everywhere we've been."

"Hayden did his best to guide us. His specialty was dreams. And for a long time, things were good." Kenny looked down. "Then a fever hit the commune. This was about two months ago. Hayden died. So did several others. That's when Elliot took over."

Lucas heard the shift in Kenny's tone. Elliot clearly wasn't someone Kenny liked.

"Hayden was a good person. Elliot isn't. We didn't realize that at first. Maybe he kept that hidden, to stay on Hayden's good side," Kenny said. "But after Hayden died, Elliot got obsessed with pushing our psychic gifts to be stronger, especially the people who could see or talk to spirits. That's what Elliot can do. He said he wanted guidance from Hayden."

"And?" Doc prompted.

Kenny sighed. "Elliot channeled what he said was Hayden's ghost. I was there. I saw it. He channeled something. But I can't swear that it was Hayden."

"Let me guess—this ghost told you to come to Mountain Cove," Doc said in a dry tone.

"Yeah. Elliot had us packing up and moving out fast enough to make your head spin. He wouldn't listen to anyone else. The people who didn't want to go got left behind. I wish to hell I'd stayed with them," Kenny said.

"How did Julie die?" Doc asked.

Kenny looked down. "Elliot wanted more power. He said it would give him 'a better connection to the afterlife' to bring back Hayden and the others. Told us that Hayden had revealed a path to him." He swallowed hard. "Elliot chose four people—Julie was one of them. He asked them to 'help' him with the ritual, that it was a real honor to be chosen. He found this house, and kept the rest of us outside, far enough away so we couldn't see what was going on."

"And?" Doc prodded.

Kenny took a deep breath. "I think he must have drugged them. We didn't know until it was over that he'd killed them. I swear, we didn't know. I wouldn't have let her go if I had known."

Doc and Lucas looked to Julie's ghost. No one could mistake the anger in her expression, coupled with grief.

"Then what happened?" Doc sidestepped any comment on Kenny's guilt.

"Everything got strange. I thought maybe Elliot had drugged all of us because it was trippy." Kenny licked his lips nervously. "We got a glimpse of these…things…that just appeared after Elliot had been in the house for a while. And then one of them forced his way inside me—"

Everything about Kenny's visage and posture changed abruptly. "And then I had a new body to wear." Red eyes flashed, Kenny's mouth twisted into a sneer, and his body tensed, ready to fight. "He told you the truth about the brand. I'm here to stay. 'Til death do us part."

Doc had a blade against the man's throat before the man had a chance to move. Its sharp edge drew blood. "I want to hear from Kenny."

Out of the corner of his eye, Lucas saw a man he didn't recognize come from the inner section of the library. He held a pitcher in one hand and something clasped in his other fist.

"Why Mountain Cove?" Shane asked. "What did Elliot intend to do when you got here?"

Kenny raised his head, temporarily himself again. "It's all about the hotel. Elliot says that Hayden is waiting for us in there, and if we work together, we can bring him back and the others as well, and we'll all live forever, and the hotel will strengthen our abilities. Even Julie. He told us that their deaths didn't have to be permanent. We could all be together again."

Lucas could see the reaction on the other men's faces. "Shit," he muttered. "This is not going to go smoothly."

He couldn't decipher the look that passed between Doc and Royston, and Lucas hadn't forgotten the issue of the request that brought them to Ansted. Neither topic seemed appropriate to discuss in front of Kenny.

Shane turned to Kenny. "What were your orders, coming here?"

"We saw you two ride by," Kenny replied. "Elliot wanted to know who you were. We knew there were people here in the library, but not why they were here. Elliot wanted me to find out."

"That's it? Just recon?" Shane pressed.

Kenny looked away. "Elliot said that if I saw a way to scare you all off, I should do it." Lucas had a feeling his orders were much less benign.

"What are we going to do with him?" Royston asked Doc.

"Well, we can't send him back," Doc mused.

"But we can try to send him on," the man in the doorway said. "I might have left the priesthood, but they say the priesthood never leaves you. We can try an exorcism, and if that fails, we can release Kenny as a mercy."

"I have the keys to the jail," Doc said. "I can add some sigils so he won't make a break for it. We can put him in there and let you do your thing."

"Happy to help," the ex-priest said. "I brought some holy water and my rosary, got the prayer book in my pocket. We're good to go."

"And when you get him locked up, we need to have a little discussion about why we're here and how, exactly, we were invited," Lucas said, glaring at Doc.

"Yeah, I figured that was coming. I promise, I'll answer all your questions."

Lucas didn't feel like chatting while Doc and the other scholar were gone. Royston cleared his throat and left the room for a while. Lucas looked to Shane.

"Well, guess we got our answer on the murder house."

"Yeah. I was really hoping it wasn't connected."

"You and me both."

3

As much as Shane knew both of them wanted to discuss the pretense that brought them to the mountain, he didn't want to be overheard, so they sat quietly until Royston reappeared to let Doc and the other scholar in after they had been gone for about an hour. The former priest spoke quietly with Royston, then headed back down the hall.

Royston and Doc came back to sit at the table.

"Alright—shoot. What do you want to know?" Doc said.

Lucas leaned forward. "Why the hell did you bring us here? Because the coven asked us to come out here months ago—before some of those 'abilities' you mentioned came to be. So, spill."

Doc sighed. "Mama Jean had a vision a couple of months ago, about two 'warriors' with special powers who could set things right. Her visions may be cryptic, but they're never wrong. Eddie got talking to a pair of those wandering IT Priests, who mentioned the two of you. Eddie felt certain you were the ones from the vision. You'd have to ask him how he got word to the witches in Bedford. I did my best to pass the word through the ghosts. Obviously it worked, because here you are."

"We're nearly ready to transfer the final materials to the hotel and move our people inside," Royston said. "But Doc says that there's something not right about the hotel's energy. We need to fix that before we get settled."

"You're going to try to...live...in there?" Shane's eyes widened in concern.

"It seems safer than trying to continue to live out here," Royston said with a sad smile. Shane remembered all the movies he'd seen where a doomed alien race packed their vast knowledge into a spaceship and sent it to the stars on the eve of their own destruction. He had never expected to confront that scenario in reality.

"If you try to live inside the hotel, what are you going to do for food and water?" Shane asked, equal parts intrigued and horrified. "What if you get in and can't get back out?"

Royston shrugged. "So far, getting in and out hasn't been a problem when the hotel is 'phased in' here."

"When it's elsewhere...I'd hate to take a chance on where or when you might turn up," Lucas added.

"Fortunately, we haven't had the need to test that," Royston replied. "We've been moving in food and water along with the archives. Doc and Eddie and Mama Jean have promised to resupply us at intervals. If or when that fails, well, we'll deal with it as it comes."

"And you're sure the hotel is empty?" Lucas pressed.

Royston's gaze shifted. "Of living people? Yes. There are ghosts. So far, they haven't bothered us. There's an exceptionally strong spirit who still seems to take his duties at the front desk very seriously. He's never bothered us. But there are parts of the hotel that don't feel comfortable, like something isn't right. Doc says there's a dark presence, but he's not sure what it is."

Shane and Lucas exchanged a glance. Shane could see that Lucas had concerns about the scholars' plans.

"That could become a problem," Lucas said, leaning forward and resting his forearms on the table. "The ghosts might not object to your coming and going—since at the end of it, you don't stay. That might change when you move in. Ghosts can be protective—and territorial."

Royston nodded. "That occurred to me. Ansted's history is worryingly full of people who were said to have 'suddenly vanished' or 'went mad.'"

"You think that might all be linked to the anomaly?" Shane asked.

"It's not too late to re-think your decision to move in," Lucas said. "I understand wanting to store the materials there. But why would you want to try to stay there?"

Royston leaned back in his chair. "We think that time works differently inside the hotel. Right now, the building phases in and out every three days. That interval has held steady for the past few years. If you're inside the hotel, what feels like a couple of hours is only minutes on the outside."

Shane noticed that Lucas seemed to tune out of the conversation for a few minutes. That usually meant he was listening to Rocky. He wondered what the elemental spirit had found important.

The shift in Lucas's expression told Shane his partner had pulled himself out of his thoughts. "The people who plan to live inside the hotel with the archives—how did you pick them?"

Royston looked surprised at the question, then resigned. "When we first started collecting materials, right after the Events, we had a lot of people who wanted to help. Over time, most of them drifted away. Now, there's a handful of us for whom the archive is our legacy, our mission."

"None of us are young, or in particularly good health," Royston said with a self-deprecating smile. "And the hospital in these parts couldn't get supplies and shut down. Doc and Mama Jean—a folk healer back in the hollow—can only do so much for us." Shane noticed that he said that last word "holler."

"Best I can guess is that four of us might have a year left, and the others maybe a little more than that."

"But inside the hotel, the time you have left lasts longer." Lucas met the man's gaze as if daring him to contradict him.

Royston didn't look away. "Yes. We figured we would go inside, set up the archives, and leave a record for future researchers. Make the most of the time."

Royston leaned toward them. "That's why we're not real worried about getting back out. If it all goes sideways...well, we were planning to take some guns and ammo with us. The hotel may be closed, but we can still check out any time we want."

"Eddie told us he was an earth witch. Is that true?" Lucas asked.

"Yes," Doc answered. "He's very powerful. Eddie and Mama Jean and I, we act as 'anchors' to help stabilize the hotel."

Lucas turned back to Doc. "You didn't call us here to be hotel bouncers. What do you know—and how the hell do you know it?"

Doc pursed his lips as if thinking about how best to answer. "There are malignant entities that have found their way into the hotel. They're parasites, not just feeding off its power but gradually poisoning it. Joseph—the scholar who used to be a priest—and I suspected one of those might be a demon. Now, after what Kenny told us, I think we can be certain of that. It sounds like the entity in the hotel duped Elliot into believing—at least initially—that it was Hayden. Probably got Elliot to allow himself to be possessed. Then once Elliot was possessed, he made sure the others were too."

"So why don't you and Joseph take care of the problem?" Lucas asked, still not mollified.

"Given the nature of my abilities, I dare not enter. Neither can Eddie or Mama Jean. And it wouldn't be safe for Joseph to force a confrontation by himself. But you could," he said, meeting Lucas's gaze.

"Why is that?" Shane felt his heart speed up. He and Lucas had intentionally avoided witches and others with magic because they feared what might happen if anyone figured out about Rocky and Quentin. If they'd have known this situation involved witches—or demons—they wouldn't have come.

It might be too late to keep their talents from being exposed, but if he and Lucas didn't like what Doc told them in the next few minutes, they could be gone by daybreak.

Doc looked Lucas in the eye. "You can see and talk to ghosts, but you can't summon them—easily. And you have a second spirit within, so you can't be possessed." He turned to Shane. "You hear the daemon song—and you have a wolf. Joseph and I have no second spirit. We could be possessed—and the result would be disastrous."

"Let me get this straight. You want me to go into a disappearing hotel and get rid of an…entity?" Lucas challenged. "How the hell am I supposed to do that?"

"I believe you have dealt with spirits before," Doc said. "Your daemon will help to protect you. And with the rituals Mama Jean and I will teach you, I think you're the only one who can do it."

"I don't like being lied to." Lucas had his back up, and Shane knew it would take some good handling to smooth his hackles.

"How could we tell you the whole truth—when you didn't know it yourselves yet?"

Shane watched Lucas's jaw work, a sure tell that he was grinding his teeth. Now that Lucas knew the full story about the archive and the scholars' plan, Shane knew his partner wouldn't walk away.

"We don't know enough about the hotel, or what we might be going up against," Lucas said finally. "Before I do anything—we need more information." He glanced toward Shane. "And it has to be something all four of us agree to," he added, including Rocky and Quentin.

"Do you have any books, diaries, or materials about the hotel itself?" Shane asked. "I'd like to read them. It would help us help you."

Royston nodded. "Yes. Give me a few minutes, and I'll get them for you."

He left them in the break room. Lucas gave Doc a look that meant he was trying to figure out his agenda.

"So Eddie is a real witch??"

Doc nodded. "There have always been witches with 'elemental magic'—people who could manipulate air, water, earth, and fire."

"Wasn't there an old cartoon about a bald kid who could do that?" Lucas quipped.

Shane rolled his eyes. "Yes. We watched the whole series while we were babysitting that witness in Dayton who ratted out the Mob's top banker. Remember? The hotel that only got four channels on TV?"

Lucas gave a sad smile. "You know, four channels doesn't sound so bad now."

"Yeah. I guess it's all relative."

"Eddie and the Mysterium are a counterbalance to the anomaly," Doc replied. "As are Mama Jean and I. But with the entity in the hotel, the skills that serve us out here would be liabilities in there."

"How does Quentin feel about that plan?" Lucas asked Shane and smirked like he could guess.

"He says I owe him a steak—or a whole deer."

"Yeah. I figured. Rocky isn't sure about the idea of hanging around either. I should take another look at that first creepy cemetery. When we passed by, I couldn't tell if they were troublemakers—or sentinels."

"They are both."

Lucas and Shane turned to look at Doc.

"You heard me say that I am a medium. I'm also a guide. I help spirits move on to where they are going."

"You're a psychopomp," Shane said. "I've read about that ability."

Doc nodded. "Very good. The ghosts in the cemetery help us watch over the hotel. They make good sentries—and they can do a lot to keep out casual trespassers. And they alert me when someone is more than 'casual.'"

"If the 'folded energy' is a natural occurrence, then why did it wait so long before it made the hotel disappear?" Shane asked. "I get the idea of psychics and sensitives locating a building where they wanted to hold meetings over an energy well, or near a helpful genius loci. But why pick a place that's unstable?"

"Maybe the psychics thought that if the Veil was thinner there, with the energies all strange, that it would help them see across to the other side. It doesn't sound like they wanted to take anything away from the anomaly. They just wanted to ride the wave, so to speak," Lucas said. "Probably what made Elliot think the hotel could bring back the dead."

"We believe that the building's disappearances and energy are being disrupted by the malignant entity," Doc said. "Ridding the hotel of the parasite energy might not make it completely solid again, but it may spread out the intervals."

"Royston told us that the area near the hotel has a reputation for people disappearing or going mad," Shane said.

Doc looked pained. "The anomaly increases latent abilities. The Spiritualists expected that and wanted it. They had studied about psychic gifts and welcomed having them manifest. They usually did fine. The people who struggled—and who disappeared and went mad—had never considered that they had abilities. Some of them believed such gifts were of the devil. They weren't Spiritualists, and they had no training and no guidance. They feared what was happening to them, and when they couldn't control the power—their abilities destroyed them."

Lucas watched him with a wary look. "I still don't like that you knew more about us than we knew ourselves."

"I'm sorry," Doc said. "We were desperate. We fear that the entity has done real damage to the hotel and that if it isn't reversed, not only will the scholars not be safe, but the hotel might become lost forever. And now, there's the added threat of the demons. We can't let them gain access to the hotel."

Lucas didn't say anything, but Shane knew that look. It might take a while for his partner to admit it, but they were staying—and Lucas intended to fight. Shane resigned himself to learning as much as he could, so he could protect Lucas—and the hotel.

"I need to be going," Doc said, and stood. "I should check on our prisoner—and bring him dinner. I'll let you know if Joseph has had any luck getting more information out of him. I will see you again soon."

Lucas and Shane sat quietly after Doc left, deep in their thoughts. Royston returned a few minutes later with a cardboard box that had what Shane thought of as a "used book store" smell of musty paper.

"This is what we have on the Mountain Cove Hotel, that old amusement park, and Eddie's place before he bought it," the scholar told them. "Some stuff about the Spiritualists, too."

Shane looked up at their host. "After the Spiritualist community disbanded, were individuals still drawn here? People interested in understanding 'the world beyond'?"

Royston perched on a corner of the table. "Sure. Some wanted to legend trip the hotel. A rumor went around for a while that there was some kind of 'magic artifact' buried in the foundation of one of the houses from the old community. Had a lot of people digging up the woods before the sheriff put a stop to it."

How did they stand being there long enough to dig something up? Shane wondered. Just riding past had given him a headache and made his wolf extremely out of sorts. *The hotel itself isn't evil. But if it has attracted other entities over the years, there's nothing to keep something evil from sneaking in.*

Quentin had thought he'd caught the scent of wolves and possibly wolf shifters. It would be good to know if they were friend or foe.

"When you and the other archivists go into the hotel, will there be anyone left in Ansted besides Eddie, Doc Swanson, and Mama Jean?" Lucas asked.

Royston shook his head. "Not that we know of. Wouldn't surprise me that there are folks at the back of the hollers that haven't come out in generations. If they wouldn't come out for movies, TV, flush toilets, and running water, they won't bother now."

Shane could grudgingly admit the logic in that.

"Doc told us that he was a psychopomp, a sort of jacked-up medium—and that he guides spirits to the afterlife. Did anyone suspect that, before the Events?" Lucas asked.

"Doc's been here a long time," Royston hedged. "It's quite a drive to the nearest hospital. Short of major surgery—the big stuff—Doc took care of it all. But everyone said he was at his best when someone was passing on. Got so that people who didn't want a priest or a minister, still asked for Doc at the end. Folks said that Doc seemed to smooth the way when someone was dying, made it easier on them."

Something's going on here that we're not seeing—and I don't think the scholars are seeing the whole picture either. Three human guardians, the cemetery ghosts, and the creatures Quentin sensed. Can't be a coincidence that they're all here near the hotel and the anomaly. But why? To keep something out—or lock it in? Maybe the anomaly and the vortex are too powerful or too important to risk allowing it to fall into the wrong hands. Or is it something else entirely?

"We usually do supper around seven," Royston told them. "Tonight is smoked venison with potatoes and carrots." At their expression of surprise, he chuckled.

"Part of that whole provisioning thing. We made sure we shot some deer, then smoked or jerked the meat so it would keep. We've had a garden since before things went bad. Plenty of root vegetables keep. Chickens and goats we plan to take with us for eggs, milk, and cheese. Brew some pretty fine beer too, if I do say so myself, and we've laid in enough moonshine for the duration." He grinned. "After all, this is West Virginia."

"It sounds amazing," Lucas replied wholeheartedly. "We haven't had a meal like that in a very long time."

Royston brightened. "You'll also have a chance to meet the rest of the team. We don't get a lot of visitors these days. They're looking forward to talking with you." He thumped the box of papers with his hand.

"I'll leave you alone to read. If the light changes, there's an oil lamp on the counter, and you're welcome to more of the tea in the big jar," he offered. "We're grateful for you coming out this way. Food and shelter are the best we can offer—for you and your horses—but you won't go away hungry."

"That's more than enough," Lucas assured him. "Thank you."

The next few hours went past quickly, with both Shane and Lucas engrossed in the materials Royston brought. Shane paged through old newspapers, yellowed letters, and a few journals kept by people who were amateur historians.

"There's a lot here. How's it going?" Shane asked after a while, taking a break to stretch and yawn.

Lucas pushed back from the table, rubbing his eyes and cracking his neck. "Slow. I hadn't really expected there to be quite so much. I found old articles about the people who died at the hotel. Interesting that someone bothered to keep them."

"So, what happened? Love triangles? Cheating spouses? Embezzlers?"

Lucas shook his head. "Surprisingly, no. The first suicide was one of the Spiritualists who founded the 1870s community, Benjamin Bowers. Part of the reason the community began to fall apart were allegations that he and the other medium, Phillip Carson, were abusing their authority and mishandling the money that was supposed to provide for the common good."

"Were they?"

Lucas took a long drink from his tea. "Carson might have been, but the coverage I've read was sympathetic to Bowers.

Maybe he was naive, or just so focused on his mission that he couldn't see that he was being bamboozled by his partner. Or, as some of the accounts hint, he might have been either a jilted lover or rebuffed one to many times."

"Trouble in paradise, huh?"

"Yeah. So when it all began to spin out of control and Carson didn't deny the allegations, I guess Bowers reached his limit. He'd been the driving force behind building the hotel. It had been his dream to fill it with seekers and students who would flock here to learn how to use their gifts or find enlightenment. He loved the place, and now it was all going to go down the drain," Lucas recounted. "Bowers walked up to the top floor suite where the view was the best and ate a bullet."

"And the other suicides? Were they related?" Shane asked.

"Not all of them." Lucas reached to riffle through the old pages. "Carson's wife collapsed from heart trouble, which she hadn't had before. The gossips thought she might have taken foxglove, unable to face the scandal. Carson slunk off. He was never prosecuted and didn't seem to feel any remorse. Sort of like those crooked televangelists who bankrupted their flocks and ran off to the islands with all the money."

"I guess that's nothing new." Shane frowned. "But the hotel's site is located on a real energy anomaly. We've both felt the psychic impact of the location. Why would a site like that draw fake spiritualists?"

Lucas let his head fall back and put his drink on the table, pausing to rub circles on his temples, as if holding off a headache. "I don't think Carson and Bowers were fake. They might have even started with good intentions. Somewhere along the way, Bowers doubled down on the mission, and Carson spotted an opportunity to line his pockets that he couldn't pass up."

"Real psychic abilities, weak personal ethics," Shane summarized. "Guess that's not so unusual."

"Carson's wife didn't kill herself in the hotel," Lucas went on. "But there were other incidents that did happen there—people who weren't famous who died under questionable circumstances. After the Spiritualist community broke up, the hotel staggered on, mostly because of its great views and the state parks nearby. Management was a mixed bag—some good and some bad. By the end, it had fallen on hard times. The woman who bought it was supposedly a seer and renowned psychic from Russia, Roza Petrova."

"Let me guess—not really Russian?"

Lucas snorted. "Not only wasn't she Russian—she wasn't really a psychic, or her abilities weren't nearly as strong as she made them out to be. It was all parlor tricks and smoke and mirrors. She was a con artist of the worst kind, defrauding widows and bilking people out of fortunes with fake messages from their dead loved ones."

"Nice," Shane replied, his voice dripping with sarcasm.

"Right? There were also rumors about her being very harsh with the staff. She brought in teenage girls from the bigger cities to work at the hotel. Then they started to disappear."

"Trafficking?"

Lucas shook his head. "Even worse. She was killing them in some sort of ritual. When they caught her, she said it was what her 'spirit guide' demanded. Before they could arrest her, she got loose and stabbed herself. Bled to death in the hotel. That was right before it closed."

"Yeah, that's not good."

"I understand why Eddie and Doc want me to go in and try to set things right. It's just a bit of a stretch from what we did with the Marshals," Lucas replied.

"Everything we've gone up against in the last four years is a stretch," Shane said. "What else is new?"

The next morning, Shane and Lucas found hot coffee and oatmeal cookies waiting for them. They had met the other scholars at dinner the night before, which was a quiet and no-frills gathering. Royston's colleagues—all men in their middle years—had been curious but welcoming, and by the end of the evening, they were swapping funny stories over a bottle of moonshine.

"You notice that alcohol doesn't hit you quite the way it used to...when we were running on our original operating systems?" Lucas asked as they gratefully swallowed down coffee.

"Burns off faster," Shane confirmed. "I can get a buzz, and then it fades quickly. I hate to think how much I'd need to drink to actually get drunk."

Lucas looked distracted for a moment. "Rocky says it wouldn't be worth the effort. Something about borrowed energy in my case, and metabolism in yours."

"Nice to know."

Lucas had gone out to check on their horses before they went to bed, reporting back to Shane that their mounts had been fed, curried, and given water. This morning they walked out to the makeshift stable to take care of Red and Shadow and thanked the man who must have drawn clean-up duty that day. Shane couldn't help noticing that there were only two other horses, although six scholars lived in the library.

"Clara—the draft horse—we bought when one of the farmers sold everything off. She pulls the wagon to help us get materials into the hotel," Dennis, a scholar and the stable hand of the day, replied to Shane's question. "Doc said he'll give her a good home when we move on. Jack," he added, with a nod of his head to indicate a bay gelding, "is on loan from Eddie. In case one of us needs to go somewhere we can't walk. Eddie will take him back when it's time."

"You're all as set on doing this as Royston?" Lucas asked. He made the question sound curious, off-handed.

"I've beaten cancer twice," Dennis said. "And that was with everything modern medicine had to throw at it. How long do you think I'm going to last with moonshine and folk remedies?" He shook his head. "I get to be part of saving some of the world's knowledge, in case there's a future. And when my time is up, I'll be with my friends." He looked away. "I lost my family in the Events. So I don't have anywhere else to be, or anyone else to be with. This is more than I could have hoped for."

Shane could appreciate that. "We're going to do our level best to make sure you're safe in there."

"Thank you," Dennis said. "We're all pretty much in the same boat. We might squeeze in a bit more time this way, and we won't be alone. I know it probably sounds crazy to you—"

"It doesn't, and it's not for us to judge anyhow," Lucas cut him off. "We've got your back."

After they tended the horses, Lucas and Shane took a brief walk around Ansted, which gave them privacy to talk.

Shane tried not to think about the eerie silence. Daily life before the Events was never silent—the distant hum of airplanes overhead or cars on a nearby highway, the buzz of air conditioning motors or refrigerators, music on the radio, a TV in the background. Here, even the nature sounds seemed muted, as if the whole area was holding its breath.

"So what do you make of Royston and his gang?" Lucas asked.

Shane had been asking himself that same question, struggling to come up with an answer. "I get why they're doing it. And—assuming the hotel doesn't just totally vanish one day—it's not a bad idea."

Lucas nodded. "Pretty much what I made of it." He hesitated. "You've been quiet about us getting invited here because of Rocky and Quentin—and me going into the hotel."

"Can I say how much I really, really don't like this idea?" Shane said, his voice sharper than he intended.

Lucas met his gaze, asking forgiveness but standing his ground. "You can. Duly noted. But there's a lot at stake. It's not just keeping the scholars safe—the entities in there could destroy the whole hotel, and the scholars and their archive with it."

"Entities, Lucas. Not necessarily ghosts," Shane emphasized. "Going in isn't the hard part. Whatever Elliot summoned is bad news—maybe a real demon. What's it going to take to get rid of the supernatural parasites?"

"Doc said that he and Mama Jean and Eddie can teach me how to dispel the entities. Rocky agrees that there's danger, but he seems to think that he and I together can do it."

"Then I'm coming with you." Shane lifted his chin and crossed his arms. Lucas's jaw twitched, a sure sign he intended to argue.

"I'm going to need you more outside," Lucas said. "The cemetery ghosts can only do so much, and Quentin might be able to call in reinforcements from the wolves and shifters."

"I don't like this," Shane grumbled.

"I know." Lucas met his gaze. "I can't say I'm thrilled, either. But I don't see another way around it."

Neither did Shane. And he figured that Lucas wouldn't commit to going in if Rocky had adamantly opposed it.

"All right," Shane relented. "But we'll be outside, watching your back."

Lucas smiled, an expression that said he understood Shane's reluctance and appreciated him going along with the plan. "I wouldn't expect anything else."

4

"I swear the energy here is starting to fuck with me," Lucas said, as they walked back toward the library. "Rocky says he's okay, but from my end, it makes my bond with him feel all jangly."

"I know what you mean. Since we got here, Quentin's been closer to the surface. I feel like the lines are starting to blur, and I'm worried, a little, about keeping him on a short leash."

Lucas frowned. "It's not too late to leave."

Shane snorted. "You heard what Doc said. You're the only one who can fix what's wrong with the hotel."

"Remember all those movies we used to watch? Being the 'chosen one' was never a good thing," Lucas replied.

"What do you need to go inside?" Shane asked, shifting the discussion. "Because if the hotel has been phasing in every three days, it should be due again tonight."

"I'm expecting that Mama Jean, Doc, and Eddie will be there with you while I'm inside. Joseph can't really do much since the demons are locked in; otherwise, we could just have him exorcise the lot of them. If Doc really is a psychopomp, then he might be able to help deal with ghosts even if his magic keeps him from entering the hotel. Mama Jean and Eddie can help you make sure we don't get blindsided by Elliot and his murder house gang."

"I'd appreciate the backup," Shane admitted. "I still don't know what kind of creatures are in the woods. I'm not going to take someone else's word on whether they're friend or foe until Quentin and I can size them up."

"Fair enough." Lucas fell silent for a while. "It sounds like Eddie, Mama Jean, Doc, the cemetery ghosts...they've all worked together to protect the hotel and the anomaly. Even so, some bad 'entities' still got into the hotel. Now those entities are harming the hotel—and affecting its energy. It would be even worse if the crazy cultists took it over. So if we can dispel the entities and get rid of the demons, maybe the anomaly can go back to the way it was, and the scholars will be safe."

"And then the guardians can protect it the way that's worked until now," Shane replied.

"We can hope." Lucas chewed his lip as he thought. "I'm going to need salt, silver, and some of those dried plants we've been gathering—the ones that are good for protection. It wouldn't hurt to have some holy water, but I don't know where we're going to get that. I'll brush up on the banishment rite—take my book with me, just in case."

"We'll back you up any way we can," Royston told them, and the other scholars nodded.

"You can help us the most by contacting Doc and Mama Jean to make sure they're with us," Lucas replied. "And if you've got any extra salt, sage, or thyme, that would also help."

"I'll check for salt and the other things you mentioned," Dennis replied. "And if we don't have it, there may still be some left over at the market. We didn't move everything out of there when they up and left."

Lucas spent that evening huddled with Doc, Eddie, Mama Jean, and Joseph, going over what he needed to know to deal with the spirits and entities. Shane sat with the scholars who specialized in folklore, trying to narrow down what kind of entity Lucas might be facing inside the hotel. Hours later, they tended their horses and thanked the scholar who was on stable duty for managing to add a dried apple to each horse's feed. Then both men finally headed to their room, exhausted.

"We think that the entity is an *ala*," Shane told Lucas. "It's a type of Slavic demon. We thought it sounded like the kind of entity that might have appealed to Roza as her abilities dimmed with age."

"Joseph went over a lot of demon lore. We can ask him if there's anything special I might need to know if it really is an *ala*," Lucas replied.

Shane helped Lucas gather what he needed from their bags.

"Once you go inside, you're going to be cut off," Shane said. "We won't know if you need backup."

"Doesn't matter if the scholars don't have the means to fight the entity and ghosts, and the rest of you shouldn't try to enter because it will fuck with your magic...power... wolf...whatever," Lucas replied with a wave of his hand.

Walking into a disappearing hotel to banish...maybe exorcise...a dark spirit scared the shit out of Lucas, and he suspected that Shane knew it. But handling the hard stuff because there wasn't anyone else to do it seemed to be the story of their lives.

Rocky, at least, wasn't quite as worried. Lucas didn't know how to feel about that. Rocky had assured him he wouldn't die so long as the elemental spirit remained as his co-pilot. Lucas feared there was a lot of potentially unpleasant territory between "being fine" and "not dead yet," and he didn't want to figure it out the hard way.

Neither man slept well that night. In the morning, Shane helped Lucas organize supplies and weapons. Iron and salt weakened or dispelled ghosts, while silver worked on many but not all supernatural creatures. Shotgun shells filled with a mixture of rock salt and iron shot would hold off a lot of paranormal predators.

"We're in luck," Shane said as he came back with two gallon jugs of water. "Joseph blessed the water." Shane held up a rosary. "And he blessed this too. So if we drop it in whatever water we want to sanctify, he thinks it will do the trick the next time we don't have a priest handy. He says he has a silver bowl and some other ritual things for you; I guess left over from his old job."

"Nice to know." Lucas pinched the bridge of his nose, staving off a headache. "We used to transport witnesses, chase down fugitives, serve warrants on mobsters. When did we become ghostbusters?"

Shane gave him a look of incredulity. "Right around the time you picked up an invisible hitchhiker, and I became a werewolf."

Lucas sighed. "Sometimes it's just a bit much, you know?"

A knock at the door made them turn, hands falling to their guns out of old habit. Royston stuck his head inside.

"Eddie, Doc, and Mama Jean are here. Come on out. We've got lunch fixed since you shouldn't go into a fight on an empty stomach."

Lucas hefted his pack and the two gallons of holy water, then followed Shane and Royston to the main lobby that had become more of a large living room.

Eddie and Doc stood with an older woman. "Marshals, meet Mama Jean," Eddie said.

Lucas sized up their new ally. Mama Jean had the sun-wrinkled skin of someone who had worked outside most of her life. She might have been in her seventies, but her eyes seemed much older. Her blue sweatshirt and jeans hung on her bony frame, practical, no-nonsense clothing meant for getting hard work done.

"Pleased to meet you," Lucas said. *What do you make of them, Rocky?*

I do not detect a threat. Their magic is very different. The woman's is most familiar as she draws on the energy of the world around her. The man who talks to ghosts feels like thunder and rushing water. The other man is fire and lightning. I do not know how else to describe them.

That's good. Thanks. Um, Rocky—going into the anomaly isn't going to fuck with your ability to keep me alive, is it?

I do not think so. I am older. It is...uncomfortable, but it does not change me.

"We'd best be going," Doc said. "Don't want to lose the light."

They rode out to the site of the hotel in the wagon, with Doc driving the draft horse and Mama Jean beside him on the front seat. Eddie rode in the back with them, but no one said much. Lucas stretched out his senses as he passed the old cemetery. This time, the ghosts did not seem to be judging him. Maybe they had decided he was another type of guardian. Or perhaps, he thought, they were focused on containing the hotel's unwelcome guests.

Lucas didn't feel the disorientation he'd experienced when they rode past the "missing" hotel, and Shane gave no indication that his headache had returned. "The energy feels different," he said.

Shane nodded. "Yeah, it's still jangled, but not nearly as

loud or painful. The horses can feel a difference, too," he added, smoothing his hand down Red's neck. Neither horse had the wide-eyed, panicked look of that first trip.

"Wow. It's really there." Shane pointed, and Lucas looked up at the large clapboard hotel. It matched what he had seen in the old photographs. The hotel stood three stories tall, painted white with a slate roof and green shutters. It looked as solid as the mountain behind it, in spite of not being there just two days ago.

Lucas tried to read the hotel with the same "ghost sense" he had used at the cemetery. The connection felt wrong, filled with static and blurry as if it were constantly in motion. Even so, Lucas picked up a darkness that sent a chill down his back. He couldn't imagine how the scholars had come and gone without noticing—or without being attacked.

Now that Lucas stood in front of the old hotel, he could sense the push and pull of warring energies—or rather, Rocky could. The cemetery ghosts kept back weaker revenants, forming a protective cordon. That told Lucas that the malignant entity must have been strong to get past them —or perhaps carried in by someone.

Rocky sensed the magics of the three guardians and the familiar resonance that was Shane and Quentin. With their protection outside and the weapons he carried with him, this was as good an opportunity as he was ever going to get.

Lucas turned and gave Shane a snappy salute, then headed up the front steps to the Mountain Cove Hotel, half expecting to fall right through stairs that were only an illusion. But his feet connected with solid stone steps, and the boards of the wide front porch held his weight.

Up close, the hotel reminded Lucas of a Victorian seaside resort he had stayed in with his parents as a child. Even then, he had been impressed by the dark woodwork, the period furnishings, and the old-fashioned wallpaper and decorations. The Victorians had an over-the-top, too-much-is-not-enough love affair with velvet, beads, fringed lampshades, and elaborate knick-knacks, and his childhood imagination made the connection with all of the ghost stories he had ever seen.

The hotel lived up to his expectations. Spiritualism either paid well, or the community's founders had come from wealth, because the hotel felt more like a resort and less like an ascetic retreat. Or perhaps the people who came to refine their psychic gifts or seek the counsel of their dearly departed relatives wanted to do so in style.

The luxurious foyer had polished wooden floors and large area rugs. It seemed to take its inspiration more from the grand lodges of the Whitneys and Vanderbilts in the Adirondacks than from monastic retreats. Comfortable furnishings in the style of Gilded Era hunting resorts were grouped for conversation in front of large stone fireplaces. Tiffany lamps cast a warm glow on side tables, while chandeliers made with elk antlers hung overhead.

Lucas stopped to take the measure of the building, now that he was on the inside. He sensed more than one faint ghostly presence at a distance, as if the spirits were holding back, waiting to see what he would do. He thought of the suicides that happened here, the missing girls, and the psychic who had willingly sacrificed those young women for her own gain.

The energies are not poisoned, but they are unhealthy. Ghosts do not have the power to do that—at least, not by themselves. Something else is here. More than one something, Rocky said.

"Welcome to the Mountain Cove Hotel. How may we be of service?"

Lucas wheeled at the sound of the man's voice, shotgun racked and ready.

The man behind the counter looked like he had stepped

out of a museum exhibit from the 1890s. The black frock coat and starched white shirt gave him a formal appearance, as did the carefully styled and Macassared hair.

"How are you here?" Lucas asked, not lowering his gun.

"Where else would I be?" The man's smile never faltered, and neither his voice nor his body language gave any hint of worry over the shotgun pointed at his chest.

He is not human. I do not sense danger from him. Curiosity. And...protectiveness. Perhaps wait to shoot him? Somewhere in their journey, Rocky had begun to acquire a dry sense of humor.

Lucas lowered the shotgun. "Let's start again. Who are you?"

The man's smile broadened. "That's more like it. I am Fenton Delacourt, your host here at the best Spiritualist hotel in the nation. At your service," he added with a shallow bow from the waist.

"I'm Lucas. I was told the hotel had a ghost problem."

Fenton looked distressed. "Oh my. I'm quite concerned to hear that sort of thing is going around—bad for business. Hard to meditate and reach your higher vibrations if you're worried about ghosts."

"My friends have been visiting. They said they saw you—and got glimpses of the ghosts."

Fenton gave him an appraising look. "Ah. The scholars. Always happy to have academics among our guests."

"They plan to become permanent residents. And...you're okay with that?"

"It's always been said that the hotel calls to those who need it," Fenton replied, his smile never slipping.

Did that include Roza Petrova, the fake Russian seer? Lucas wondered. *Or Bowers, the doomed co-founder of the failed Spiritualist community?*

"I'd like to have a look around," Lucas said. "I can help

restless ghosts move on. Send troublesome spirits elsewhere. There's something here that is…twisting…the hotel's energy."

Fenton frowned. "We do not speak of that," he warned. "Some things are best not mentioned."

Lucas hadn't come to argue with…whatever Fenton was. "I promised my friends that I would look around and make sure everything was ready for them. I mean no harm to you or the hotel."

Fenton gave Lucas an incisive stare. "I believe you."

He can sense me, Rocky whispered in his mind.

Is he afraid of the entity?

It would appear so. Or perhaps, cautious. I pick up traces of a dark power, but I can't locate it yet.

Keep trying. I think Petrova might be the key to this.

Lucas hefted his bag and headed toward the public areas on the first floor and from there, to find the basement. He had a map provided by Royston, and he knew where the scholars had stored their archive materials. Based on that, he had already decided to save the top floor and Bowers for last. Given how much Bowers loved the hotel and the community, Lucas didn't think he was the source of the problem.

The hotel's large open dining room continued the sense of rustic luxury. The tables were set for dinner, with glassware and china place settings that glittered, not a speck of dust in sight. Lucas reached out to assure himself that the pieces were solid, although how "real" they were was a matter of debate. Here inside the hotel, at least, things were real enough to be dangerous. Lucas needed to remember that.

"What'll you have?" a familiar voice hailed him from behind the elaborate bar.

Lucas turned to see Fenton drying glasses, wearing a

bartender's vest. The mirrored backbar reflected the glittering lights of the chandeliers.

"Fenton?"

"Can I make you a cocktail, sir? Or perhaps pour a few fingers of good scotch?"

Fenton either didn't recall their earlier conversation or had a reason for pretending not to. *Or maybe he's not the same Fenton. Rocky?*

I can't say for sure yet. Proceed with caution.

Lucas felt a prickle on the back of his neck that usually meant a ghost. He turned slowly, shotgun down but ready if needed. A faded figure sitting by the grand piano caught his attention.

"That's Irene. She doesn't bother anyone," Fenton said. "Been here for a long time. She just doesn't want to go home."

Lucas moved closer slowly. The woman's dress looked to be from the early 1900s, and she sat at a table near the piano, turned as if she were listening to music only she could hear. She didn't seem to notice him or to have heard the conversation. Lucas wondered if she was a "repeater"—a ghost whose energy had faded so much that it was like an image on a video loop, without sentience or the ability to react.

He turned away, willing for now to let Irene stay. When Lucas looked back toward the bar, Fenton was gone.

"Like that's not creepy at all," he muttered under his breath.

Lucas spotted a set of nondescript double doors in the back of the dining room used by the waitstaff. He slipped through them into a service corridor that ran behind the public rooms, linking them all to the kitchen and storage rooms for tables, chairs, and other materials.

If the stories about Roza and her bloody obsession were true, Lucas doubted she carried out her murders in places where guests were likely to hear or interrupt. Even the hotel staff might have objected to seeing some of their own gruesomely killed. That meant looking for the basement.

Lucas had a pack of matches and a candle in his jacket pocket and a lantern with extra candles in his pack since he had been unsure what he might find inside the hotel. By the time the hotel closed—and disappeared—in the 1920s, it had electric lights. Lucas hadn't been certain that the version that reappeared would be the most recent, or always be the same version, for that matter. He had learned the hard way not to take chances.

An unlocked door marked "*Basement*" led off the service hallway. While Lucas felt glad he didn't need to shoot the lock to get in, he noticed marks that suggested it had, at one time, been padlocked shut.

He opened the door and found a light switch. To his relief, a bare bulb glowed to life over the stairway. The cement stairs and metal pipe railing had clearly not been meant for guests. A musty smell rose from the bottom, the smell of damp concrete, mildew, and mold.

The main room at the bottom held the boilers, furnace, electrical panel, an ancient generator, along with pipes, ductwork, and conduits. As with the rest of the hotel that Lucas had seen thus far, the lack of dust and cobwebs made it look still in use. Lucas moved carefully, sweeping the room for threats, but saw no one. A dark hallway led off from one side.

"You really shouldn't be down here."

Lucas wheeled, only to find Fenton, dressed in workman's coveralls, standing by the furnace where, seconds ago, there had been no one.

"What are you?" he demanded, refusing to lower his shotgun this time.

"No one goes down the hallway," Fenton continued as if he hadn't heard the question. "It's off-limits."

"Oh yeah? By who? Madame Roza?" He headed toward the hallway, and Fenton moved toward the doorway as well.

Lucas turned the shotgun toward the mysterious man. "I don't want to shoot you—but I will if you get in my way. What's in the hallway that I'm not supposed to see?" Fenton didn't answer. Several possibilities churned in Lucas's mind, and he took a chance.

"That's where she kept the girls, isn't it? They died back there. And I bet some of them never moved on. I'm not here to hurt them. I want to set them free."

For the first time, Fenton's expression changed from the pleasantly unreadable mask Lucas had seen before. He actually looked worried. "It's dangerous. She likes to visit them."

She. Madame Roza—or whatever she's become—is still torturing those poor spirits.

"I intend to stop her," Lucas told Fenton, who might be an unlikely ally but was the only chance for backup he had. "Can you warn me if she comes?"

For just a second, Fenton seemed frightened. *If he's somehow tied to the hotel itself, and Roza—or whatever "malignant entity" she's become—is feeding off the ghost girls, then maybe she's also leeching off him.*

"How about you just bang on a pipe if she shows up? That way she won't know," Lucas suggested.

Fenton nodded and moved back toward the boiler. Lucas found the switch for the second hallway and made his way forward carefully, feeling all his senses go on high alert.

Be careful. The energy in this area is unnatural. Something has tainted it. This is not part of the energy of the mountain, or what you call the anomaly, Rocky warned.

The first door opened into a stockroom filled with old tools and handyman supplies. The second held spare parts and odd bits of lumber and pipe. Lucas kept his attention fixed on the last door, which from its placement on the hallway, suggested it led to a somewhat bigger room. As with the main basement door, it looked as if a padlock and plate had been removed.

By now, his ghost sense screamed in the back of his mind, and gut instinct told him to run. Rocky held steady, so Lucas kept moving forward. The lights overhead flickered, and the hallway grew steadily colder as he moved farther from the main boiler room. At first, Lucas had chalked that up to being away from the heat from the furnace, but now he knew it was a sign of strong ghosts nearby.

He stopped and pulled out a canister of salt from his bag, then laid down a line across the hallway so nothing blindsided him from that direction. The corridor ended in a wall to his right, which meant he didn't worry about anyone coming at him from there. Then Lucas readied his shotgun and swung the third door open.

The stench of old blood and decay assaulted him. Lucas reached for the light switch and recoiled as the single bulb revealed the horrors inside.

Two filthy mattresses lay on the floor, soiled with blood and dark stains Lucas didn't want to ponder. A pair of manacles lay on the floor, and he saw a ring set into the stone wall where the chains could be fastened. A dented bucket stood in the corner, and a side table held what appeared to be surgical instruments. A gilded triptych hung high on the far wall as if to oversee the carnage.

Lucas swallowed back bile. He didn't need an imagination to fill in the details of how Roza kept herself busy.

The light flickered once more, and the air grew impossibly colder. Lucas felt a slight breeze where there shouldn't have been any.

"I came to set you free," he said to the empty room, knowing that spirits lingered even though he couldn't see them yet. "What she did to you was evil. I'll deal with her later. But if you're stuck here—I can send you on."

One by one, three faint images struggled to be seen. Lucas relied on his ghost sense, and that helped him make out more details. The three spirits were all teenage girls, perhaps seventeen or eighteen, he guessed. They looked emaciated, making it even more difficult to judge their ages. He felt relief that they had not manifested with their death wounds. Containing his rage already took a lot of his focus.

Lucas quickly set out four candles and connected them with a circle made from salt and other protective powders. He spoke the words to the litany Joseph had taught him to help stranded spirits find peace, turning clockwise as he did so to light the candles. Both Doc and the former priest had assured Lucas that the ritual elements actually helped to focus and transmute power and weren't just for show.

As Lucas lit the last candle, he felt sure that the energy in the room had changed. The air felt thick with power, and even the ghosts seemed to sense the shift.

Rocky?

Keep going. The doorway you are opening has nothing to do with the mountain. Something held the spirits here. Send them through, quickly.

Lucas had memorized the second incantation, words of blessing and release. "The path is clear, the way is shown. Leave the fetters of your ties here behind, and follow the light that calls you. Go to your rest, and be troubled by this world no more."

The energy in the room roiled as if two unseen powers struggled against each other in a clash that made his head pound and his stomach lurch. In the distance, he heard the clang of metal on metal. A pinpoint of bright light opened like a glowing spark in the middle of the room. Primal caution made him back up, even as the three ghostly women moved toward the glowing ember, which expanded in a single flare, forcing Lucas to shield his face.

When his vision cleared, the spark and the ghosts were gone. On a hunch, he strode across the small room and took down the triptych.

Lucas!

Rocky's warning made Lucas turn just in time to hear the clang of Fenton's wrench against the pipes and see a dark cloud rolling down the hallway toward him, blotting out the light.

Lucas turned and fired the shotgun into the dark mass. A shriek of rage and pain echoed from the walls. He fired again, and the cloud dispersed, but he knew it would be back. Reloading took seconds, and then Lucas dug in his pack for more supplies.

The cloud is not one being.

What does that mean?

I sense an angry ghost and several other energies that are not human—and never were.

Demons

Not daemons.

No, demons...infernal spirits from Hell?

I do not know of Hell.

Just my luck to get an agnostic daemon for a co-pilot, Lucas thought. *What kind of harmful not-human energies are there?*

More than we have time to discuss.

Lucas thanked all the video games and horror movies he and Shane had watched. The writers had done their homework, although they had probably never thought they would be writing a post-apocalyptic primer for hunting monsters. Those memories, coupled with the intense briefing by Doc, Eddie, Mama Jean, and Joseph, would have to suffice.

Lucas grabbed a piece of chalk from his bag and drew protective sigils on both walls on his side of the salt line, knowing Roza and other entities were gathering power once more.

"Rocky—can you talk to Fenton? Do you know what he is?" Lucas muttered, raising his shotgun once more.

I have been trying to figure that out since we entered. He is not exactly a daemon.

Lucas fired into the cloud, but this time, the black smoke parted, letting the shell pass through harmlessly.

"Fuck!" He changed his aim, swinging the barrel to one side at the last instant, and the entity shrieked as the salt and iron pellets ripped through it, then vanished.

"If he's not *exactly* a daemon, then what is he?" Lucas growled.

He is the soul of the hotel.

The soul?

That is the closest word in your thoughts. Such things can occur—

Save the explanation for when we're out of here. Can he help us?

Perhaps.

Lucas dug weapons and ingredients for the incantation out of his bag. "Gotta do better than that, Rocky. I don't want to be the next new ghost."

He pulled out the silver bowl Joseph had given him and hurriedly shook in holy water, as well as cinnamon and dried thyme the ex-priest found in an abandoned convenience store, and mint gathered along the roadside. As the black smoke began to build again, Lucas relit two of the candles he had used in the other room and pulled out a photograph from the box of memorabilia the scholars kept.

"Roza Petrova! Show yourself in your true form!" He dipped one corner of the photograph into the mixture in the bowl.

The smoke suddenly cleared. In its place stood an old

woman. Age lined her face and silver streaked her dark hair, but the strong chin, high cheekbones, and sharp nose still held a cold beauty.

"Put that down!" she commanded, pointing imperiously at the photograph Lucas held.

Lucas had both his ghost sense and Rocky's energy to take the measure of the spirit. Roza was strong enough to appear nearly solid, and even at a distance, Lucas felt her power.

"Why did you summon the *ala*?" Lucas shot back. He held up the triptych, which confirmed what Shane and the scholars had guessed.

"I outlived my family, my lovers, my children," the ghost said, her Russian accent—real or affected—still thick. "And then, worst of all, I outlived my magic. Do you know what becomes of old women who have no one to care about them?" Her eyes narrowed. "They become prey."

"So, you decided to summon a demon and become the predator instead?" The blood-soaked room behind Lucas started to make sense in an awful way.

"I did what I had to do." Roza lifted her head.

Lucas's abilities let him see the ghost clearly. Rocky's power enabled him to see the shimmer of the creature beside her, glistening like black oil, a form that was in no way human. It reminded him of Shane's vision at the murder house and the black ooze that had filled Elliot after the sacrifices. A nighthawk perched on her shoulder, a creature the folklorists had said was likely a *zwodziasz* in disguise, a type of imp.

"And so your *ala* and your nighthawk helped you lure the girls, which you slaughtered to keep your bargain? What did you get out of it?" Lucas had suspected the triptych factored into either her control over the demons or sealed her deal—regardless of which it was, destroying it wouldn't be in her favor. From the way Roza's eyes tracked the relic in his hand, Lucas knew he had her weak spot.

"I would not have to die," Roza replied, and her voice still carried a sense of aristocratic condescension.

"Because you feared what awaited you?" Lucas couldn't help being curious.

"I am a survivor," Roza told him in a strong voice. "What I had to do, I am not always proud of, but still, I did what needed to be done. I am in no hurry to be judged."

Lucas wondered what crimes Roza had committed before coming to Mountain Cove, what in her history had created a woman of such indomitable will that she defied both Heaven and Hell.

"I came here, to the hotel, near the end of my powers. For several years, everything was very good. I liked it here. Then, my abilities began to fail. Some of the guests complained that I had not 'performed' to their liking—as if I were a circus animal for their amusement." She sniffed.

"The hotel was also dying, running out of visitors. Bowers's suicide was a blood sacrifice, although he didn't mean it to be. He gave his life wishing for the hotel to continue. The hotel itself might close, but the energy of the mountain was eternal. I realized I could tap into that current, extend my powers, buy myself time. I called on the *ala* for help, offering more sacrifices if it would keep me strong." Roza's voice held no trace of remorse.

"You became a parasite," Lucas replied. "To save yourself, you nearly destroyed the hotel and seriously fucked with the energy of the mountain."

She shrugged. "What is the saying? Ah, yes. Needs must, when the devil drives."

In the distance, he saw Fenton blocking Roza's escape—and another man Lucas could not see clearly, an older gentleman in a Gilded Era suit and top hat. He wondered how much the salt and iron he had fired into the dark cloud had drained Roza and her demons. Curious as he was about her story, Lucas had no intention of letting Roza regain her mojo.

Roza's eyes narrowed, and Lucas felt pressure against his temples as if she was trying to force herself inside his mind. The nighthawk took flight, and the demon slithered forward, both impossibly fast.

Lucas plunged the photograph into the mixture with one hand, as he smashed the triptych against the stone floor with the other. A red flame rose from the bowl of consecrated ingredients, and the broken relic burned with an eerie green fire.

He braced himself to feel the nighthawk's claws, but instead a transparent, glittering scrim of power rose from the salt line, stopping the imp like a bird flying into a glass pane. The demon backpedaled. Lucas felt Rocky's energy surge at the same instant that the salt circle flared with light.

"Roza Petrova—I abjure you and your dark instruments of infernal power. Your power here is broken, your spirit is banished, and your essence is anathema. Depart and never return."

Roza threw back her head, shrieking as the demon began to devour her and the nighthawk pecked out her eyes. The demon swallowed her whole like a huge snake, then consumed the imp as well, and went up in a surge of blindingly bright green flames.

When Lucas dared to open his eyes, blinking against the burn-in of the demon's flare, the hallway was empty, except for Fenton and the other ghost, who still remained as sentinels.

Are we safe? he asked Rocky silently, carefully gathering up his materials. Lucas removed the soggy photograph from the bowl, and then dropped the broken relic and the photograph into the rusted bucket from the other room, squirted some lighter fluid, and tossed in a match.

Rarely had he felt such satisfaction over a trash fire.

The Fenton-entity and the ghost do not appear to mean us harm, Rocky said.

Good. I've kicked enough ass for one night.

Technically—

It's just an expression, Rocky.

Lucas had expected Fenton and the well-dressed ghost to vanish while he packed up his gear, but to his surprise, they remained on guard as he walked down the hall toward them.

"Thank you," he said. "I have the feeling you helped keep that from being worse."

Now that he could make out the ghost's features, Lucas recognized him from the pictures. Benjamin Bowers, the ill-fated co-founder of the Mountain Cove community, the man who loved the hotel so much he chose to die there rather than see his life's dream fall apart.

Bowers looked Lucas up and down, then gave an approving nod and vanished.

"I guess he's one of the hotel's permanent residents, like Irene?" he asked Fenton as the coverall-clad version of the mysterious host walked back toward the stairs with him.

"Yes, he and a few others. They will not harm your friends. Now that the creatures and the one who summoned them are gone, the hotel—and the energy of the mountain—can heal," Fenton said. "We look forward to having the scholars move in. It will liven the place up," he added with a wink and a smile.

"I need to get back." Only now did Lucas remember the warning that time inside the hotel passed at a different rate than in the outside world. How long had he been in here?

"I'm afraid you can't leave just yet," Fenton said as Lucas reached the bottom of the steps. "Roza and the demon forced the hotel to phase before its time—that's the shudder you might have felt."

Lucas vaguely remembered feeling a disconcerting lurch back in the service hallway but had attributed it to the overall weirdness of the hotel itself.

"Am I trapped here? I thought you wanted the scholars to move in?" A surge of panic made Lucas's heart pound. Nice as the hotel was, he had no intention of becoming a permanent guest.

"Now that the parasite is gone, the hotel will adjust," Fenton told him. "Give it a couple of hours, and one of us will let you know when it is safe for you to leave. We are in your debt," he said, making that shallow bow again.

"In the meantime," Fenton suggested, "go see my counterpart in the bar. The liquor is quite real—and we have a nice selection. On the house."

"Are you really the soul of the Mountain Cove Hotel?"

Fenton gave an enigmatic smile. "That is as good a description as any. A combination of the residue of power left behind by many psychics who were even more talented than they expected, the mountain's unique energy, the ley lines beneath, and a man who believed in the hotel with so much passion that when he died, his essence sustained it."

"I'm pretty sure, after everything, I could use a drink," Lucas replied. "Thanks for having my back."

"Thank you for setting us free. You are not the usual visitor yourself."

"I may have been told that a time or two," Lucas replied with the twitch of a smile, and a friendly mental nudge to Rocky. "I'll be in the bar."

5

Shane watched Lucas enter the Mountain Cove Hotel with a spring in his step. It was just like his partner to manage some swagger, even when heading into a building that wasn't always real.

Ever since they had faced down playground bullies together in elementary school, Shane and Lucas had been a team, and that meant Shane had been worrying about his best friend nearly his entire life. Knowing that the worry was returned didn't blunt the awful feeling in his gut.

He forced himself to turn away as the door clicked shut behind Lucas and looked at their new allies. "What now? Do we just stand here until he comes back out?"

Eddie chuckled. In his dark, old-fashioned suit, he really did remind Shane of a vampire, although seeing him in bright daylight disproved that theory. Still, Shane wondered if Eddie affected the look and mannerisms for protection, or whether they were just a remnant of days gone by.

"Now we make sure nothing goes in after him," Eddie told Shane. "Tell me—does the energy feel different from when you came?"

Shane shoved down his worry and forced himself to focus on what he heard in the song of the mountains' elemental spirits, and what Quentin sensed around them. When he and Lucas had ridden into Ansted, the mountain's energies had felt so jangled that he could barely function, giving him a headache and making Quentin surly.

The pain and extreme uneasiness he and Lucas had felt when they passed by the empty hotel site on their way into town was gone, perhaps because the hotel was back. Just in case, Mama Jean had given them each spelled charms to wear. Lucas's hung from a strap around his neck. Shane's charm hung from a long leather cord that would still fit if he shifted to his wolf form.

Shane still felt off—the melody that he heard from the genius loci of the hills remained jumbled. Though where before it had sounded to him like many songs sung over top of each other, now the tunes were more like a round, interweaving and overlaying without discord. Quentin still paced, expecting an attack, but he didn't whine and scratch and growl in Shane's mind like a canine alert for imminent danger.

"It's better than it was," Shane replied. "Is it the hotel being here that makes the difference?"

"To a large part," Eddie said. "When the hotel phases out, the vortex and anomaly are out of balance, which causes discomfort for anyone with psychic sensitivity. We think the malignant entity's effect on the mountain's energy just makes it worse. The energy in this place has always been different. That's what called to so many people with special gifts."

"The hotel was supposed to be an anchor, built into the mountainside." Mama Jean spoke up. She brought a willow broom with her, along with a large basket and a cloth-tied bundle. While Shane watched Lucas head into the old building, Mama Jean walked a few dozen paces down the road and began to sweep the surface clean, murmuring under her breath as she worked.

"Something's put the energies all catawampus," the witch said. "Like the hotel took sick. You get an infection, and it gets in your blood, makes it bad. There's something that's got into the hotel, infected its energy like bad blood. Fix the sickness, and the hotel won't ever be regular normal, but it will be back to its old self."

Mama Jean turned away and began to scatter a mixture out of the cloth bundle over the swept-clean area of the road. She did the same to the rest of the section of asphalt in front of the hotel, bidding her companions to move out of the way, until she had swept and sown a stretch that covered the whole area.

"There," she said, dusting off her hands. "That should help keep out any riff-raff that want to make trouble. Ward away bad intentions." She cocked an eye at Shane. "You have that charm I gave you?"

"Yes, ma'am," Shane replied, pulling at the neckline of his shirt to reveal the collar. "I made sure Lucas was wearing his too, before he went in."

She nodded, apparently satisfied. "Good. Don't take it off."

Whatever hesitation Shane might once have harbored over magic had been dispelled by the realities of the world after the Events. He didn't have to understand Mama Jean's protections to believe they provided another layer of defense.

Doc Swanson remained in a spot where he was nearest both the old cemetery and the hotel itself. He stood absolutely still, eyes closed, as if he had taken root.

"What's he doing?" Shane asked Eddie.

"Talking to the ghosts, asking them to help us protect the

hotel, sending them out as scouts. He'll be like that the whole time we're here. Don't worry—he's fighting his own war, we just can't see it."

Mama Jean walked along the forested edge of the road, scattering the mixture from her bag and dropping small charms made from sticks, leaves, string, small bones, and pinecones, another level of warding to keep away troublemakers.

"Mama Jean understands the plants and roots—how to make medicine or poisons, how to use them to cure or kill. How to blend them to gather energy or scatter it," Eddie answered Shane's unspoken question.

He pointed to the hotel. "You and Lucas are sensitive to the elemental spirits. I perceive the energies of the deep earth. So I see a vortex here, all those subterranean currents fountaining up. But when a vortex happens in the same place as an unusually strong area of elemental magic, you get an anomaly. And that anomaly has been stained by whatever sickness has befallen the spirit of the hotel itself."

Shane had so many questions he wanted to ask. But his head had begun to throb just from being so close to the powerful energies in the cleft that held the hotel. Quentin seemed closer than usual to the surface of his consciousness, and the longer they stayed, the more restless Shane's wolf became.

"I can sense the wolves," he murmured, looking into the forest that stretched from the edge of the road to the horizon. He walked toward the shoulder of the asphalt, careful not to interfere with Mama Jean's wardings and listened to the songs of the genius loci, and to the sounds of the forest, which to Quentin were like a native tongue.

The rush of sensation through his bond with Quentin nearly overwhelmed Shane. Sight and sound took on a new level of definition, a whole new range he had never experienced as a "normal" human. He'd heard of people describing an acid trip as "expanding consciousness" and dismissed the description as junkie justifications. Now, he wondered if those altered states came close to the torrent of new colors, sounds, smells, and detail that assaulted him.

He turned back to Eddie. "There are other beings like me out there. Regular wolves. Wolf-shifters. Werewolves."

Eddie nodded. "The wolves began gathering after the Events as if the mountain called them home."

Shane concentrated, stretching out his senses in ways he had never tried before, both his ability to hear the songs of the daemons and his new wolf-mind.

"It glows." Shane's soft tone of wonder elicited a smile in response from Eddie.

"Beautiful, isn't it? Especially the first time you can see it as it really is."

In his mind's eye, Shane saw Mama Jean's protections as a shimmering spring green ring of light. He hadn't seen Eddie do anything witchy, but the area beneath their feet and the bedrock of the mountain behind the hotel had a deep blue inner light. Doc's magic looked like a spiderweb of golden strands. When Shane looked into the forest, he saw quicksilver flashes like light on water, and he knew in his bones they were the creatures that were not entirely normal. Creatures like him.

Then Shane looked at the hotel. A confluence of energies seethed and roiled beneath and around it like a private storm, a mingle of blue and green, shot through with an odd thread of gold. But a shadow cast across the hotel itself, dark despite the brilliance of the power surging around it, silent despite the cacophony of the anomaly's song.

"I see the hotel—and the stain. That's what Lucas needs to

fix?" Shane wasn't sure his partner knew he had signed on for something so big.

"He need only remove the source of the poison," Eddie replied. "When that is done, the hotel and the anomaly will heal itself."

Pain spiked through Shane as if someone had rammed an ice pick through his skull. He cried out and folded in on himself as he collapsed. Eddie grabbed his arm, helping to break the fall.

"Shane!"

Eddie's voice sounded distant. Images came fast, like a TV montage almost too quick to follow. Elliot, back at the murder house, sacrificing the first victims, calling the demon, opening himself to possession. At the settlement in Hico, same ritual, new victims, only this time, the demons filled more bodies as Elliot burned the sigil-lock into their skin, trapping the demons inside and condemning the hosts to unending torment.

Strong hands gripped Shane's shoulders, shaking him. The voice calling to him wasn't Lucas's, and it took Shane time to remember the man in the strange, old-fashioned clothing. In his mind, Quentin snapped and paced, restrained by the thinnest, fraying control.

"I'm okay," he managed, as memories flooded back.

"A vision?" Eddie surmised.

"Yeah. Unpredictable—except for the part where it's always at a bad time." Shane let Eddie help him to his feet and guide him to sit on the back of the wagon while the earth witch dug out a chunk of dried meat and a full wineskin from a bag.

"Always eat after magic. Replenishes what the power takes out of you," Eddie advised. He waited as Shane followed his advice, even though Shane wasn't entirely sure he could keep the food down.

"I saw the cultists—the ones from Hico," Shane said as soon as he could manage his thoughts. "Elliot and Kenny weren't the only ones who were possessed. I think they all are now. The demons took their bodies and…hijacked their abilities. Demon witches," he warned, with all the urgency he could muster. "They've got magic—and demon strength. And Elliot branded them, so exorcising the spirits won't work. We're going to have to kill them all."

Eddie opened his mouth to respond, then shut it without saying anything and raised his head, as if scanning for danger.

Shane felt the mood shift between one breath and the next. In his mind, Quentin's hackles rose, and the wolf began to growl. Doc Swanson did not move, except to raise both hands from his sides to bend at the elbow, out in front of him. Mama Jean lifted her head as if she could smell trouble on the wind. With a crafty smile, she went back to walking and singing, tossing out more of the mixture from her bundle from time to time.

"Get ready," Eddie warned.

Shane forced himself to stand, taking a position beside Eddie. "Ready for what?"

The area where Mama Jean had sown her protective mixture flared with white light. Although the barrier absorbed the attack, Shane sensed the hostile magic skirting around the edges of their defenses, looking for a weak spot.

"They're here. The cultists," Eddie said.

Quentin surged against Shane's inner restraints, eager to get out and join the fight. Shane had to focus his will on keeping Quentin inside.

We don't know what we're up against, Shane argued with his wolf.

Enemy. Fight.

They're demons and bad witches. They could set our tail on fire.

Not if we bite first.

Down, boy. Maybe later. Can you sense the others like us, in the forest?

Yes. They are coming.

Here?

To fight. We go too?

Not yet.

No fun.

Shane was still adjusting to being able to communicate with his wolf side. Most of the time, Quentin rested quietly inside Shane's skin without causing trouble. Now, it took conscious thought to keep him restrained.

"How can I help?" Shane asked Eddie.

The wardings flashed as the attackers tried their energy against it, reminding Shane of electric bug zappers. Streaks of green light showed where the demons lashed out at the protections, but Mama Jean's perimeter held. She had stopped walking, but the song and chant never paused.

"Call to the creatures. You're one of them. Bring them in behind the troublemakers," Eddie suggested.

"I've never done anything like that. I've only had Quentin for about a month."

Eddie raised an eyebrow. "Interesting. You have surprising control for one so newly turned."

Shane wasn't willing to share that Rocky and Lucas helped to anchor him and guided his transition. He felt their absence keenly and glanced up at the hotel as if he could will Lucas to join them.

"I'll try. Quentin wants to make some noise. Maybe this will keep him happy."

Those other creatures—can you draw them closer? Box in the bad people?

Quentin gave a satisfied growl. *Let me out, and we howl.*

Shane did not want to shift, not here without Lucas and

Rocky to help. But the longer the cultists assailed their protections, the more Shane could feel his precarious control begin to slip. He wasn't sure he trusted Quentin—trusted himself—without his partner to anchor him.

A song is just a different kind of howl, Shane thought, seizing on an idea. He took a deep breath to center himself, trying to ignore the impatient wolf that paced in the back of his mind. Instead, he remembered what he had seen earlier, the flashes of silver amid the forest. He focused on those quicksilver images and leaned into the songs of the mountain daemons.

Shane had never tried to influence the songs he heard. Now, he sent a rush of images, hoping that the elemental spirits behind those songs were as sentient as Rocky. He pictured the hotel under attack. And then he turned it over to Quentin and brought his own wolf song, letting it surge up from deep inside.

He felt…something. The darting silver flashes stilled, listening. A howl sounded in the distance, then another, and another, until the forest resounded with the howls, yips, and barks of creatures that were more than they appeared. And Shane felt the song shift as if the mountains howled along.

The quicksilver flashes became a tide, coming to hunt. *It's working.*

"They're coming," he managed. The cost of the effort hit him, and Shane fell to his hands and knees as his whole body trembled, fighting to keep his wolf inside his skin, struggling to remain human and in control.

The temperature dropped steadily, and Shane wondered if Doc had called in the ghostly cavalry. The bug-zapper bursts of light against the wardings had slowed. Beyond the protections, Shane heard growling, the snap of teeth, and human screams. He thought he caught a glimpse of gray spirits, beyond the curtain of magic that shielded the hotel's defenders.

"Let's see if I can shake things up a little," Eddie muttered, and Shane felt a surge of power flare as the witch gathered his abilities against the attackers. The ground under their feet trembled, and then beyond the green perimeter, rocks lifted into the air and pelted the attackers as Eddie lunged forward, hand outstretched, palm open. The cultists scattered, shouting as a hail of rocks hit hard enough to draw blood. And then, silence.

The wardings glowed solid, but the attacks abruptly stopped. The creatures were out there, Shane could feel their power bleeding through his weakening control, but they had backed off, keeping their distance.

Shane heard a rumble like thunder, despite a clear blue sky. Without warning, hot agony surged through Shane as if every bone had been crushed at once and his body were being turned inside out, skin flayed. He gasped and panted, barely holding onto consciousness let alone keeping Quentin under control. But his wolf had retreated, whining in fear and pain.

Mama Jean's song rose in defiance, and Shane recognized the old hymn about blood and spirit and redemption. He shivered as the legion of ghosts swept past them, flowing back to Doc and then beyond, seeking shelter in their graves.

What the fuck is going on? The wardings are supposed to keep out magic.

As quickly as the assault came, it vanished. It took all of Shane's strength to keep himself up on his hands and knees and not just collapse onto the roadway. Quentin had retreated to the back of his mind, but Shane knew there was a moment there when his control hung by a thread.

That was close. Too close.

He froze. The Mountain Cove Hotel had vanished.

That's what we felt, the hotel ripping loose and floating away to wherever it goes. God, I thought it might kill me. If it was that bad out here, what was it like for Lucas, inside?

Shane turned to help Eddie, who had collapsed beside him. The witch was pale, and one cheek was scraped where he had gone down hard against the road, but he was breathing and had begun to move.

Fuck. What do I do now? How do I get Lucas back? When the hotel returns, will he still be alive?

Eddie's hand closed around Shane's arm, startling him. "Help me up," the witch said, sounding a little woozy. Shane pulled the other man to his feet and supported him with an arm around his shoulders as Eddie swayed.

"Day-um. Just as I sank my power down into the ground to shake things up for those cultists, the hotel went and pulled a runner." Eddie looked up at the huge bare spot on the mountain where the building had been not long ago.

Shane didn't feel too steady himself, not after the whiplash of energies that had zinged through his mind and body, or the tug of war with Quentin. Now that the hotel was gone, the energy felt more like it did when he and Lucas first rode by the site, jangly and fractured, although the charm from Mama Jean definitely helped.

Eddie nodded, taking a step to indicate that he could stand on his own. Shane let his arm drop but remained watchful.

"The cultists, they're gone?" Shane asked, looking to Mama Jean and Doc.

"They're gone alright, but it wasn't us who scared them off, not completely." Mama Jean stood with both fists on her hips, staring at the mountain as if she meant to give it a piece of her mind.

"This might have been a scout team, sent to see what new capabilities you and your partner brought. They didn't figure on the hotel throwing in a surprise of its own," Eddie added.

"What about Lucas?" Shane asked, fixing his attention on the empty space as if he could will the building back into place. "Is he..."

"We won't know until the hotel comes back," Mama Jean replied. "Best you can say is that he went in ready to fight a supernatural enemy, and that's more than others have."

"But the hotel had just reappeared. It hasn't been here for three days yet. It shouldn't have been ready to phase out. It changed its schedule." Shane felt like the hotel had somehow violated an unspoken contract.

"We never have known what set the frequency of the hotel's coming and going," Doc said. "Might be that the hotel does as it pleases."

"You talk about the hotel like it's sentient." Shane fought down fear and panic. *I knew I should have gone in with him. I was hardly useful here, and I almost couldn't control Quentin. At least if I'd stayed with Lucas, someone would have his back.*

"There's been a lot of debate over the years about that," Eddie responded. "No one knows for sure. Me, personally? I think it's become more than just a building. Can't tell you why or how—just a hunch."

"How do we know when it will come back?" Shane had no idea how to mount a rescue if the building wasn't there anymore.

"We don't," Mama Jean said.

"Lucas is in there!"

"And there's not a blessed thing we can do for him right now," Mama Jean replied. "We're just going to have to wait."

Shane looked around himself, then back at Mama Jean. "This area is still warded, right?" She nodded. "Then I'll wait here. Should be safe enough."

"The cultists will be back," Doc said.

"Then I'll shift and sleep in my fur. I'm not leaving without Lucas."

A silent conversation seemed to stretch between Doc and Eddie in a shared glance and Doc nodded. "How about I take the wagon to Ansted, bring back bedrolls and food and firewood, and we set up camp, right here, for the duration? Mama Jean can patch up the warding after Clara and I go out, and after we come back in."

Eddie nodded. "I agree. We shouldn't leave the hotel unguarded, and we have no way to know when it will return. We'll keep a vigil until it does."

"What about the road?" Shane asked belatedly. "We've cut off the town if anyone needed to get through."

Doc chuckled. "We've been out here for most of the day, and there hasn't been a soul yet that needed to go through. Don't think you need to worry about that." He headed toward where he had left Clara and the wagon. "I'll be right back. You just sit tight."

Eddie sat down cross-legged on the roadway, facing the forest. Shane sat next to him. Mama Jean went to fix where the edge of the warding got broken by Doc's departure, then walked the perimeter again, singing and chanting.

"Doc and Mama Jean are from around here," Shane finally said, breaking the silence. "So they can't compare how their magic was before being near the hotel and afterward. But you came from somewhere else. You said this place drew you here. Did it change your magic over time?"

Eddie stared off into the woods, although Shane couldn't see anything out there except trees at the moment. "It's a gradual thing," Eddie said, finally. "Like the way you adjust to shorter days and longer nights in the winter. Sometimes, you don't even know anything's changed until all of a sudden, something you never used to be able to do just opens up as a possibility."

Eddie shot him a side glance. "I imagine for you, with

your bond with your wolf so new, the anomaly is making it hard to stay in control."

Shane hesitated, then nodded. "I came way too close to losing control of Quentin."

Eddie looked back toward the woods. "That's one way to look at it, I guess. What would have happened if he'd forced you to shift? Would he have attacked one of us? Eaten someone? Run off into the forest to chase the demon?"

Shane looked down at his hands. "I don't know. That's what scares me. But...I don't think so. He wanted to howl and rally the other creatures." He had never shifted without Lucas and Rocky to back him up, and they had promised that they wouldn't allow him to become a threat.

"He's still you," Eddie said. "Maybe a little more impetuous. If you don't lose your man-mind when you're in your fur, then it's really about gaining new senses from the wolf, not losing who you are as a human."

Shane sat with that for a moment. The hybrid shifter-werewolf that bit him had been the product of government experiments to create a super-soldier. It had been following orders when it attacked because Shane was firing on the rogue scientists and the dark witch that were the creature's masters. *He didn't attack me at random. He was still on task, carrying out his mission.*

That hadn't occurred to Shane before, and he almost gasped with the realization. *Those soldiers didn't already have the ability to hear the daemon song. They didn't have Lucas and Rocky to keep them on track. And even so, they followed orders.*

Maybe Quentin won't go feral, even if the mountain's magic breaks my control.

In his mind, Quentin raised his head from his paws, gave Shane as close to an eye-roll as a wolf could manage, and went back to sleep. Shane resolved to rest while he could. Perhaps he had gotten accustomed to the energy around him, or maybe Mama Jean's charm had even more power than Shane expected. But it seemed to him that the uncomfortable dissonance had eased, and the remaining jangle did not seem as painful.

A few hours later, Doc returned with the wagon, laden with supplies. Mama Jean fixed the wardings after he entered, and Doc drove Clara and the wagon into the center of the warded space.

"Got everything we might need to sit this out for a few days," Doc told them. "Food, water, whiskey, coffee, blankets, bedrolls, and a couple of tarps, in case the weather turns." He started unloading the firewood, as Shane and Eddie rose to help him.

The sunset painted the sky in rich shades of orange and pink. Shane and Doc got a fire started, while Eddie and Mama Jean sorted through the provisions to roast a simple supper of potatoes and sausages in the fire, with some dried fruit for dessert and moonshine to top it off.

Shane glanced over his shoulder at the empty mountainside, but the hotel had not reappeared. He shoved down his worry for Lucas, hoping that his partner would be safe and be able to get out of the hotel, and he wondered if Lucas's mission had been successful.

"You said that we didn't really run off the cultists in their full power," Shane said when they had eaten and were still seated around the fire, each with a cup of moonshine. "If what we did wasn't enough, how can we beat them when they return?"

"We don't know how it would have ended if the hotel's phase-out hadn't run them off," Eddie said after he'd taken a sip of his drink. "More of the creatures turned out this time to lend a hand because of you."

"More ghosts too," Doc added. "Your partner had a talk

with them, I guess," he said with a look toward Shane. "That made an impression."

"If Lucas can heal the hotel, then its energy begins to heal too," Mama Jean said, picking a stray bit of meat from between her teeth. "We don't know what that will mean in a fight, but I wager it's something."

6

"I'm so sorry you didn't have the chance to experience dinner here with us," Fenton said from behind the Mountain Cove Hotel's front desk. "Come back any time."

Lucas hefted his gear bag and headed for the hotel's main doors, wondering how long he had been gone in "real" time. The hotel hadn't stayed its usual three days before vanishing —although barkeeper-Fenton assured Lucas that was more a fit of pique on the part of the establishment than a matter of habit.

Now, he wanted to get out while the getting was good and move the scholars in before the damn place picked up and left again.

He flung open the front door—and nearly collided with Shane, who approached the entrance with his gun up, ready for a fight.

"Whoa! Hold up. Don't shoot! It's me," Lucas said, putting his hands up in surrender and staying perfectly still.

"Lucas?"

"It's me—and Rocky too," Lucas replied. "Don't believe me? Ask Quentin."

Shane watched him warily, then his expression went blank for a moment, and Lucas knew his partner was checking with his ride-along wolf. Shane blinked, and smiled broadly, pulling Lucas into a backslapping hug.

"What the fuck, man? You scared me half to death. This was supposed to be the Overlook Hotel, not the TARDIS."

Lucas grinned at the geeky reference. "Yeah, well, let me tell you—it's even bigger on the inside." He hurried Shane down the steps, not willing to trust the hotel to stay put.

"You decide to take up camping?" Lucas asked, looking over the scene in front of the hotel.

"We had no idea when the hotel would come back, or how long it would stay when it did," Shane answered, nervously glancing over his shoulder as if the big building might be listening. "And we fought off some demon-witch scouts right after you went in, so we didn't want to leave the place unprotected for them to get in."

"Scouts?"

"I'll tell you all about it," Shane said, clapping him on the shoulder and looking ridiculously glad Lucas was back. "We have food. Come on and eat. That way you can tell everyone what the hell happened in there."

Lucas wondered whether the top-shelf scotch bartender-Fenton had served him was real, since he didn't feel any buzz.

It was real while you were inside the hotel, Rocky supplied. *If that helps.*

Lucas gratefully accepted the greetings of Doc, Eddie, and Mama Jean, as well as a plate of eggs and sausage and a cup of fire-brewed coffee. They held off questioning him while he ate. The sun had just risen above the treetops, and Lucas wondered how long he had been gone.

"About twenty-one hours," Shane answered his unspoken question. "You blinked out around nine o'clock yesterday morning, and got back right around six this morning."

Lucas just stared at him. "You've got to be kidding. That means I'd only been inside for an hour before the hotel vanished?"

His three companions nodded. "Shit. Time does move differently in there. With everything that happened, I was sure it had been at least three or four hours before the hotel vanished."

"You felt it?" Eddie asked, curiosity sparking in his eyes.

"It's not something I could have overlooked," Lucas replied and finished up the rest of his food. "I just didn't know what it was until the hotel wouldn't let me leave."

Once he had a refill of coffee, he recounted his story. The others listened without interrupting, fascinated at his tale.

"So you got rid of the ghosts and two demons and stopped off at the bar for cocktails?" Shane questioned.

"Fenton makes a really nice martini," Lucas said with a shrug. "You know how long it's been since I bellied up to a bar and ordered a drink?"

Shane's skepticism turned wistful. "Yeah—probably since that hotel in Cleveland on our last witness assignment."

Later, Lucas intended to have a long talk with Rocky about the "feel" of the hotel's energy. Just with his mostly human senses, Lucas thought the atmosphere inside felt lighter after Roza and the demons were gone.

"I sensed when you dispelled the ghosts," Doc said, after taking a long draught of his coffee. "Thank you for sending them on."

"It was past due. They had suffered far too much." Lucas figured his experiences would be new fodder for nightmares.

"The hotel packs a wallop if you're outside when it comes or goes," Shane said. "But the 'jangle' is a lot less since you got rid of the entity, and with Mama Jean's charms. And it's definitely better when the hotel is 'home' than when it's away."

"So Bowers has become a guardian," Eddie mused aloud. "That's interesting. Then again, perhaps he loved the hotel more than anything else in his life. So maybe it's not a stretch."

"He didn't want to leave," Lucas spoke up. "Neither did the other ghosts, like Irene. They can move on whenever they choose."

"Where did the demons come from?" Shane asked. "Did Roza summon them?"

"Spirits are around us all the time," Mama Jean replied. "Roza might have done a spell—she seems like the type. But if she was willing to kill those poor girls, then maybe those dark spirits were with her for a long time, and she just fed them enough to take shape on their own."

Lucas stretched and moved to refill his coffee. "When we've got the demon-witches handled, the hotel is ready for the scholars. Fenton confirmed that they were welcome to move in permanently—that they'd 'liven up' the place."

"Fenton sounds like an interesting guy," Shane observed. "How can a hotel have a soul, anyhow?"

Mama Jean gave him a thoughtful look. "You know, we talk about the spirit of the mountains, and the valleys, and the rivers. You can call them daemons, or genius loci, or elementals, but most folks call it the soul of the place." She leaned against the wagon, drinking her coffee and turned her gaze out over the horizon.

"I don't know if all those are the same energy. Don't know if it rightly matters. If you can have a daemon with you," she said, looking straight at Lucas, "and a wolf in you," she added with a glance at Shane, "then why can't the hotel have a spirit of its own? Especially in a place with such unusual energy."

That might be as close to an answer as we ever get, Lucas thought. *And if the hotel is happy, that's all that matters.*

Doc straightened and set down his coffee cup. "They're coming. The ghosts have spotted them."

"How many?" Eddie asked, as they all stood and quickly gathered up their things, leaving the fire burning within the circle of rocks that contained it.

"Two dozen, maybe a few more," Doc replied with a far-off look as he listened to his ghostly scouts.

"I've been thinking about the fight yesterday," Eddie said, as Doc retreated to the place he stood before, calling to the ghosts, and Mama Jean made a circuit to strengthen the wardings. "And I have some ideas to serve up something the demons won't expect—and maybe keep us from getting knocked on our asses again."

"How come everyone has a costume since the Events?" Lucas grumbled. "The IT Priests. Those knights we met up with. Now we've got gray-robed dark lord wannabes."

"You're just jealous," Shane teased, trying to hide his nervousness. "I mean, we used to wear our Fed suits."

"Yeah, and good riddance. Because if there's one thing I don't need after a fuckin' apocalypse, it's a suit coat and necktie."

Ominous figures stood outside Mama Jean's perimeter, massing silently in a creepy attempt at intimidation. Lucas felt like he'd been dropped into one of the video games he and Shane used to play to pass the time while they were babysitting witnesses. *Except if that were true, I'd have a way-cooler outfit.*

"You want to do it now, or later?" Lucas asked his partner.

"Might as well be done with it," Shane replied and headed off behind the wagon. A moment later, Lucas heard the heavy clink of a belt buckle against wood as Shane threw his clothing into the bed of the wagon, staying where he could shift to his wolf form with a bit of privacy.

Quentin padded out, looking rather pleased with himself, and let out a long, loud howl. He walked up to stand beside Lucas, who reached down to scratch him behind the ears. Quentin rumbled in warning, a familiar response to Lucas's intentional provocation.

Other howls answered. As long as the wolves and the other shifters remembered which side they were on, Lucas welcomed all the help they could get.

The loud crack and flare of light made Lucas jump as the cultists lashed out with the demons' power and their own hijacked magic against the protective wardings. Red fire streaked across the spring green glow of the protections, like bleeding gashes.

He could see the ghostly protectors Doc Swanson rallied. The spirits wove their way among the cultists, passing right through some of the robed attackers. Those that could manifest with more strength hurled rocks, clawed at arms and faces, or pushed and shoved, shrieking and keening in an ungodly caterwaul sure to raise gooseflesh and take a toll on concentration.

Quentin howled again, and Lucas imagined his partner as a wolf general, directing the shifters, calling them to battle. Lucas glimpsed dark blurs of motion, attacking behind the lines. That forced some of the cultists to turn their attention away from the warding, to avoid being mauled. Unfortunately, more robed attackers stepped up to take the place of those who tired or fell to the shifters and were-creatures.

"Remember—the real people are in torment, with demons

locked into their flesh," Eddie called out. "Killing them ends their pain. It's a mercy."

Mama Jean walked slowly around the perimeter, chanting and singing. Lucas wondered how long she could sustain the wardings.

Not forever. I believe that is their goal—to exhaust her and make the walls fall.

How can we help?

My energy sustains your life. I can spare only small amounts without harming you. I can help you see more, if that would help. And you have your weapons. Be ready.

Lucas already had his shotgun locked and loaded. He added a couple of knives from his gear bag and stuck a Colt 1911 into the waistband at his back.

"Can I shoot through the warding, or will it ricochet?" Lucas called out to Mama Jean. He hated to interrupt her chant, but getting shot by his own bullet wasn't high on his list.

"The warding is one-way," Eddie answered for her. "We could step through it if we wanted—wouldn't recommend it. Fire at will." He grinned. "Give me a minute to do something, and that way you won't waste bullets. I've got a few tricks they haven't seen yet. This ought to get their attention."

Green and red flashes lit the forest like cursed neon lights. Eddie found the place where the cultists threw their energy hardest against the wardings, looking to make a weak spot. He raised one hand to focus his magic, limned in a blue glow as his power rose.

Eddie called out a word of power and clenched his fist. The ground beneath the witch-demon's feet trembled and then gave way, creating a sinkhole that sprawled for several yards and sent many of the attackers falling into the void. Those lucky enough to jump out of range now found themselves with a yawning chasm keeping them from getting close to an entire stretch of the warding.

"And I hope it goes all the way down to Hell!" Eddie shouted for good measure. Lucas figured that if the brands kept the demons from being exorcised, they might also trap the demons inside the corpses of those who fell into the pit.

While the attackers' attention was on the sinkhole, Lucas started shooting. He braced himself, ready to duck on the first shot, but when the rounds passed cleanly through the warding, Lucas grinned.

"Just like shooting womp rats," he muttered. When this was over, he and Shane would have to do another "re-watch" of their favorite movies—by taking turns recounting the storyline, complete with all the dialogue and details they could remember.

The wolves harried the attackers from behind the lines, crowding them toward the sinkhole or into the steady fusillade Lucas kept up. Some of the demons turned to lash out with their power against the shifters or ghosts, with little effect.

Eddie set his sights on another area farther down the perimeter, where the demon-witches continued their attack on the glowing green protective barrier. He repeated the spell, creating another sinkhole and sending more of the cultists tumbling into the opening.

Eddie staggered and would have fallen if Lucas hadn't grabbed him by the arm.

"Thanks," Eddie managed, looking exhausted by the effort. "Even with the vortex to draw on, that kind of magic kicks my ass. I don't want to undermine the road and make us fall in too, and I'm not keen on setting off a rockslide." He sank to the ground. "I'm going to need to catch my breath before I do something else."

Lucas stepped in front of him, protecting the witch, and

resumed firing. He had no idea what Shane conveyed with his howls, but with the way the sounds varied, he knew some kind of communication was taking place. The wolves and shifters certainly had no trouble staying clear of Lucas's shots.

Lucas knew that the cultists couldn't all evade his bullets without making a full retreat. He varied his targets, never shooting twice into the same area, hoping to keep them on edge and kill as many as he could.

As the hours passed and the siege continued, Lucas knew they needed to find a way to up their game. Reinforcements had arrived for the cultists, but the defenders had no one else to call on since the scholars had neither the magic nor the weapons to provide backup.

Quentin's "voice" sounded strained, but he kept up the yips and barks that coordinated the wolves' assault. Mama Jean looked haggard and had stopped pacing to rest on the edge of the wagon, working up a mixture of some kind from her large basket and the cloth bundle inside. The wardings had held so far, but Lucas didn't know how long they could go on like this.

A flash of red, brighter than most, seared across the warding, and a figure surged forward, trying to cross the protective border. Quentin crossed the distance in a few leaps before Lucas had even focused on the threat.

"No teeth!" Lucas shouted, just as Quentin attacked since the last thing they needed was a newly turned demonic were-witch. Quentin's jaws snapped shut, and his claws slashed down through the seeker's shoulder. The demon-witch sent a streak of energy crackling toward Quentin. The wolf dodged, but the strike caught his hindquarters and sent him tumbling, with smoke rising from his fur.

Lucas shot the demon-witch in the head, then ran closer and swung his knife to decapitate the corpse. Mama Jean hurried to fix the breach in the warding, with Eddie right behind her, drawing from his magic to open a fissure beneath the feet of the cultists crowding forward to force their way through the protective barrier.

"Shane!" Lucas ran to check on his partner. Shane had remained in his wolf form, despite the injury. The smell of singed fur made Lucas choke. Quentin permitted Lucas to check on the injury to his hindquarters, which left a red, angry burn.

"You okay?" he asked, hoping that with tempers battle-short and a fresh wound, Quentin didn't forget his human side.

Quentin's yellow eyes met his, and the wolf gave a solemn nod. "Okay. We'll patch you up once we're done here. Maybe Doc knows a good vet," Lucas teased, relieved the damage hadn't been worse.

Quentin managed to curl his lip at Lucas's joke. The wolf tried to stand, but his injured leg gave way, and he collapsed, panting at the pain.

"Tell him to stay in his wolf form for a while," Eddie called. "His metabolism is higher from his shifter magic. He'll heal faster."

"You hear that?" Lucas asked. Again, the wolf nodded, then tossed its head toward the warding, as if to shoo Lucas back to work. Then Quentin let out a long howl that sounded like a battle cry.

Lucas crossed back to where Eddie and Mama Jean knelt over a pottery bowl filled with a mixture of fragrant plant leaves and powders, as well as other ingredients he didn't recognize.

"I'm just mustering some more power to help hold the gates," Mama Jean said, glancing up when Lucas joined them. "My mother, and her mother, and her mother's mother were all witches who are buried in these hills. We swear an oath to come if our descendants call on us with this ritual. They'll help carry me through."

Lucas could see that the effort of sustaining the wardings had gone hard on the older woman. A glance at Doc told him that rallying the ghosts was causing him strain.

"Can you and Doc team up? Would that help?" Lucas suggested. "Share the load and all?" He turned to Eddie. "Do you think there's any way what you can do with the vortex might be able to connect with my daemon and the anomaly to do more together than we can alone? I've still got a fair amount of ammunition, but it won't last forever."

"Maybe," Mamma Jean said. "Might be worth a try." She took her things over to where Doc stood, and Lucas turned his attention back to Eddie.

"Like she said, can't hurt to try," Eddie replied. "There are more of them coming. We can't do this all night, and we don't dare let them storm the hotel."

"How long until their reinforcements get here?"

Eddie's expression went blank while he checked with his magic. "Maybe half an hour. I'm sorry I can't just open up a pit big enough to swallow them all, but that would probably take us with it, along with half the mountain."

"That's okay," Lucas assured him. "But maybe we can gather enough help to take them all out at once."

"You know, if it doesn't work, we'll have probably run ourselves dry," Eddie warned.

"If it doesn't work, we'll have sped up the inevitable, but we're going to run out of juice sooner or later," Lucas said, sparing a worried glance toward where Quentin lay partly sheltered by the wagon, trying to rest and heal. Clara, the cart horse, had either been remarkably trained or—more likely—was under a calming spell to not react to the strange noises and lights all around them.

"Are you two scheming something?" Mama Jean asked

when she returned from conferring with Doc. "'Cause me and Doc have our part ready—and maybe a bit more, if things turn out."

"We're ready," Lucas said, and Eddie stood, still looking worn but at least on his feet. Quentin wasn't asleep, and he gave a yip of encouragement.

"Whatever you see out there, don't let it bother you none," Mama Jean said. "There are even older protectors in these woods than the granny witches and the shifters—things as old as the daemons and the vortex. They don't like to be woke up, but I think we've got good reason to do it."

She walked back to Doc, and Lucas looked at Eddie. "You have any idea what she's talking about?"

Eddie's eyes narrowed as he thought. "They say there are some real strange creatures in these forests, much stranger than shifters. Most people think they're just folktales, but then again, they say that about magic too."

"Let's do this." Lucas took a deep breath and let it out again, refusing to think about how tired he felt. He reloaded all his guns and checked the supply of remaining bullets. It should be more than sufficient—unless the demons just didn't stop coming. Lucas had never tried to pair his connection to Rocky with a witch's magic. Hell, he'd only had Rocky onboard for a short time, and until now, they had tried hard to stay clear of both other hunters and people with magic, for fear of how his new co-pilot might be perceived. When Shane got turned, that gave the partners even more reasons to stay away from anyone who might be able to read the truth about them.

If they had known in advance about Eddie, Doc, and Mama Jean, Lucas wasn't entirely sure he and Shane would have come, fearing the worst. But they had found acceptance and support. Lucas wasn't naive enough to expect that from everyone, but it did mean he and Shane needed to have a discussion—assuming they lived through this fight.

"We need a physical connection. Put your hand on my shoulder," Eddie instructed. "And I'll do the same."

"Feels like senior prom, all over again," Lucas said, as he found himself at an awkward arm's length from Eddie.

Eddie chuckled. "Not much of a dancer? That's alright. We don't have to move. Just don't break the connection, got that?" Lucas nodded. "So go call up your daemon, and I'll tap into the vortex—and we'll see if we can wake up the neighbors."

Lucas shut his eyes and focused on his link with Rocky. *Can you do anything else with a little boost from Eddie? Because we're stretching pretty thin on our own.*

I can't leave your body without killing you. But perhaps I can see if any others of my kind can hear me.

What about the anomaly? I feel like we're on top of a huge source of energy and we aren't using it.

The anomaly is unstable. But now that the hotel is back, and healing...let me see.

Lucas felt vulnerable without a gun in his hand, as the cultists gathered along the warding and resumed their assault.

He caught motion out of the corner of his eye and saw that Shane had dragged himself behind the wagon to get dressed. He emerged in human form, limping toward the gear bag to get his gun and shotgun, noticeably dragging his wounded left leg. Shane caught his eye and gave him a nod and a cocky grin. Moments later, steady gunfire provided cover for Lucas and the others to make their move.

Lucas's hand tingled where he gripped Eddie's shoulder as if he brushed against a live wire. He felt Rocky's energy shift the way it did when he "spoke" to the other elemental spirits in the parks, mountains, and special places where the genius loci were strongest.

The tingle grew into an uncomfortable burn, as Eddie channeled the vortex's vast energy. Lucas felt Rocky draw back from the other daemons and wrap his essence around the bright blue flow of Eddie's earth magic. That core of energy rose through Lucas's body from the soles of his feet, burning like fire in his veins, filling him with a rush of power and a flood of images from eons of awareness.

Lucas felt the energy build until pain filled him, and his body seemed too small to contain what they had summoned. The staccato beat of gunfire melded with his own scream and Rocky's stern voice as the power tore through him and then released, sending a shudder through the ground that made him stagger and that sent trees swaying and rocks tumbling.

He opened his eyes and looked past the green light of the warding. Fewer of the robed attackers remained, and those who did battled ghosts, wolves, and creatures the likes of which Lucas had never seen.

One of the beings resembled horror movie hellhounds—a fierce black dog-like monster the size of a pony, with red eyes and wicked fangs. In the distance, a faceless white creature with the shape of a large man lumbered toward the cultists, who scurried to get out of his way.

Two more creatures came into view, both nearly the height of a man but moving all wrong. One had a muscular profile, with hunched shoulders and a larger than normal head. It waded in among the attackers, swinging its huge fists, smashing them out of his way. The other looked like a sci-fi movie alien, with a robed body and a pointed cowl or helmet where its head should have been, glowing a lava-red color from within.

Lucas's head throbbed, and fever burned through his

body. He heard Rocky shouting in his mind as his knees buckled, and then he fell to the ground, landing hard on his ass, the connection with Eddie broken. He barely helped to break Eddie's fall as the man collapsed next to him, unconscious.

Shane kept firing. *How many of them are there?* Lucas wondered, wincing as the noise assaulted his aching head.

Doc and Mama Jean were leaning on each other, and while they might have been sharing their energy and magic, it looked to Lucas like they were holding each other up.

Beyond the shimmering wardings, some of the demon-witches lobbed balls of energy that impacted and spread like a wound over the green protective curtain of light, while others attacked the monstrous protectors Doc and Mama Jean had raised.

Eddie groaned, and Lucas checked on him, finding the witch awake and trying to sit up. Lucas steadied him and went to get them both water from the provisions in the wagon.

"This isn't looking too good for our side."

Lucas shifted, and that brought the hotel directly into view. "I should have thought of it before," he muttered to himself. He let go of Eddie and lingered just long enough to make sure the other man could stay upright.

"Stay here." With that, Lucas sprinted for the steps to the hotel and sincerely hoped he had not read Fenton wrong.

"Welcome back to the Mountain Cove Hotel. Lovely to see you again," Fenton greeted him from behind the front desk.

"There are dozens of crazy demons out there who want to take over the hotel and use its power," Lucas explained breathlessly. "We've been fighting them all day, but we're losing. There are too many of them. We've done everything we can do—including call up the Old Protectors—but it's not enough. If those demon-witches get inside, it'll make Roza and her *ala* look like a Sunday picnic by comparison—and they'll tap into the vortex and the anomaly, which will make them damn near unstoppable."

Lucas hoped he had made his case. Fenton needed to understand the risks. Outside, Shane's sustained gunfire sounded like a rapid heartbeat.

"Another threat to the hotel, you say?" Lucas spun to see Benjamin Bowers's ghost descending the broad staircase. "That's unacceptable. We just got rid of that Russian fraud and her unsavory companions."

"If you and the hotel can do something—anything—to defend yourselves, now is the time," Lucas begged. "Because my friends and I are half-dead, and we can't go on much longer. We need your help."

Bowers went to the front window, looking out over the battlegrounds, and down into the valley. Lucas remembered that the man had been a powerful psychic, back in his day, and that he had loved the hotel more than his own life.

"I have not seen the Old Protectors go to war in a long, long time," Bowers mused. "The snarly yow and the White Creature do not rouse from their slumber easily." He turned toward them. "You know what we need to do," Bowers told Fenton, who nodded soberly.

"Go back to your people," Fenton said, looking at Lucas. "We appreciate all that you have done to safeguard the hotel. Gather your friends and have them amplify the song of the mountain in their own way, and together, we will defend her."

Lucas had no idea what Fenton was talking about, but he nodded. "I'll tell them. Better do what you're going to do soon. Good luck."

With that, he headed back outside, running as fast as his exhausted body would go to rally the others. Lucas quickly relayed what Fenton and Bowers said and saw a mix of resignation and hope in his companions' faces. They all knew that if this didn't work, they would die, the hotel would be overrun, and the scholars and their archive would be doomed.

"What did he mean—amplify the song as we know how?" Shane asked, finally falling back from his non-stop fusillade, although he kept his gun loaded and his eyes on the cultists who remained at a careful distance beyond the warding. Lucas could see that the green glow of the protection had faded badly. They were nearly out of time.

"Our magics," Eddie said. "Tune into them, in our own ways. Like we've been doing, only with the hotel joining in too. Throwing everything we've got at the cultists, all together."

"It could burn us up," Mama Jean noted. "You need to know that."

Doc Swanson smiled sadly. "Doesn't really matter if those demon-witches get through, we're burned up anyhow."

"I'm in." Shane met Lucas's gaze, and Lucas swore he saw a flash of wolf yellow in his blue eyes. He knew from the set of Shane's jaw that his partner had made up his mind.

"Hell, yes," Eddie said, looking exhausted but resolute.

When I told you that you might become immortal, I expected you to still have a body, Rocky warned. *I cannot promise what I can do if you burn up.*

Understood.

They turned back to Mama Jean. She flashed a broad, snaggle-toothed grin. "What are we waiting for? Let's throw down and be done with this nonsense."

Lucas looked back at the hotel. *We're ready,* he thought, wondering if Fenton or Bowers could read his mind.

He and the others formed a circle, joining hands. Lucas focused on the warmth of the skin of the two people on either side of him, on the regular rhythm of his breath—in and out—and on Rocky, a silent, powerful presence.

The irony of surviving the Events only to be killed in a battle between a cursed hotel and a bunch of demon-witches didn't escape him. Surely they hadn't come through so much for it just to end here.

He snuck a glance at Shane, whose expressions he knew as well as he did his own. Lucas could read the tension in his partner's shoulders, in his response-ready stance, and the squint of his eyes. The others looked equally stressed and resolute.

Now, a voice said in his mind, a voice that wasn't Rocky. Lucas braced himself, surrendering to fate.

A blast wave of power rushed through Lucas like he was trying to contain the whole of the ocean within himself. The storm surge of energy blew his abilities wide open, full strength. He saw the restless ghosts of the mountain, and he heard the songs of the genius loci from all the neighboring hills and valleys. This was the anomaly and the vortex mingled, and it felt like mainlining the raw, primordial forces of creation.

Lucas tightened his hold on the hands on either side of him, not daring to open his eyes. The shred of consciousness he retained that was still Lucas knew that the currents flowing through him were not meant for fragile human comprehension.

He heard the crash of falling trees and the roar of rock-slides, wrapped in the howl of the wind as if the Titans themselves had awakened. As quickly as the blast began, it ended. Lucas swayed on his feet like he had been leaning into a strong wind that suddenly vanished. Their joined hands remained clasped white-knuckle tight, holding them up.

I'm alive. At least, I think I am. Heartbeat. Breathing. Holy shit —I survived!

We're still intact. Let's not do that again, Rocky said.

Lucas opened his eyes, almost afraid to look. The green warding was gone, and none of the gray-robed cultists were anywhere to be seen.

"Look." Shane pointed, and his voice held a combination of awe and fear.

All of the trees in a semi-circle moving out from the cleft of the mountain lay flattened, pointing away, as if Lucas and his friends were ground zero. *Like that meteor strike in Russia, a long time ago.*

He felt a tug and realized he still had his companions' hands trapped in his own vice grip and loosened his hold with a chagrined smile of apology. They all looked as shell-shocked as Lucas felt.

A glance over his shoulder revealed Fenton and Bowers standing on the hotel's wide porch. Fenton met his gaze, smiled and nodded, and then he and the ghost went back inside. Lucas wondered how long the hotel would hang around this time. Did it need to retreat somewhere to recharge? Or was its true home here in the cleft of the mountain with the anomaly and the vortex?

"Well, that's sorted," Mama Jean observed, dusting off her hands. "Don't think we'll see any more trouble, not for a while."

Doc Swanson nodded. "I suspect that you're right."

Eddie stared out at the flattened trees. Lucas wondered how much the land witch's experience had differed from his own since Lucas was linked to the daemon of the mountain, while Eddie's connection was to the forces of the earth beneath.

"It's a lot to take in, all at once," Eddie said. "Going to need to sit with it for a bit, I think."

Lucas agreed whole-heartedly. The others began to make their way back to the wagon, where Clara the cart horse stood, patiently waiting. Lucas wondered what spell Mama Jean had put on her, because she seemed to be taking this whole thing far better than the rest of them.

"You okay?" Shane asked, giving Lucas an appraising look.

Lucas managed a shrug. "We're still here, alive, in one piece, not burned to a crisp or stark-raving mad. I'll take it as a win."

Shane gave an unsteady laugh. "Yeah. Just another day on the job, staring down the maw of the universe."

"Getting to be the new normal," Lucas said, slapping him on the shoulder, a gesture that said everything they didn't need words to express. *We're alive. I'm glad you made it. Scared the fuck out of me. Damn, that was one hell of a ride.*

When they reached the library, the scholars rushed out to meet them, all of them asking questions at once. Lucas and the others did their best to answer, but all they could really manage was to assure the academics that the threat had been eliminated, the hotel was safe, and that Fenton confirmed that they were welcome to finish moving in.

"If you need me, you know where to find me," Doc said, leaving Clara and the wagon for the scholars to use and heading home on foot after bidding them goodbye with a wave.

"I'll be in my garden," Mama Jean added. "You take care moving into that hotel, you hear me? This rescuing stuff is hard on my joints." With that, she reclaimed her horse from the stable and rode off.

"You held up your end of things," Eddie told Lucas and Shane, shaking their hands. "Not bad for being the new kids," he added with a grin. "I imagine I'm going to have hell to pay to untangle some of the ley line energy back at the Mysterium, but it's a small price for setting things right. Stop by if you're in the area again. Preferably when you don't need to save the world." He headed for the stable to get his mount.

"We have a pot of rabbit stew ready for dinner, with biscuits and baked apples," Royston said. Lucas could see the scholarly curiosity that burned within the other man's eyes, but thankfully Royston held off with his questions for now. "And I imagine you'll need some moonshine to take the edge off. You both look like you've gone six rounds with a drunk grizzly bear."

Lucas and Shane looked at each other in the same instant, synchronicity born out of years on the road together, and then both of them broke out in unstoppable laughter.

"Sometimes you eat the bear," Lucas managed, laughing so hard it hurt to breathe as all the tension of the last several days finally reached a breaking point.

"And sometimes the bear eats you," Shane finished, tears coming to his eyes as he shook with the laughter that purged away the hardship, exhaustion, and terror.

Royston just stared, then finally gave a what-the-hell smile. "Come on in. I guess you've got quite a tale to tell—after you get fed and cleaned up. And if you're still not up to snuff then, the moonshine'll put you right."

7

"What the hell is a snarly yow?" Shane asked as they helped the scholars load the last of their boxes into the wagon. A few days had passed since the battle, which gave Lucas and Shane a chance to heal and rest before heading back on the road.

"It's a big black dog—somewhere between a hellhound and a grim," Royston replied. "Those Old Protectors you say Mama Jean and Doc conjured up; they're the legends people tell their children at night to keep them out of the woods. That White Creature is one of them—big, burly shape but covered with smooth white skin and no features. The other two would have been the Grafton Monster and the Flatwoods Creature. They're West Virginia's versions of Bigfoot."

"They were real," Shane protested. "At least, real enough to do damage."

Royston shrugged. "Don't get my academic friends started on a debate about the nature of reality," he warned with a smile. "It could be that Mama Jean and Doc created a mass illusion. Or maybe they really did wake up ancient spirits to rise and protect the land. There are plenty of legends to that effect. Then again, maybe they were real because you believed in them—sort of like a tulpa."

"I don't think I have to tour Eddie's Mysterium in order to see the laws of the universe turned inside-out," Lucas muttered. "If someone told me the story we just told you and I hadn't seen it for myself, I'd have said they were tripping balls."

"I'm quite looking forward to getting to know more about this Fenton character—in any and all of his roles," Royston said. "But just in case he decides not to share his bar with us, we're taking an ample stash of moonshine and our still." He grinned. "It pays to be prepared."

Lucas and Shane offered to help the scholars unload at the hotel, but Royston assured them they could handle it, and Shane noticed that Lucas didn't insist.

"Thank you," Royston said, shaking their hands. They had already said goodbye to the other scholars, whom they had gotten to know from shared meals and help with research. Shane wished them well but felt equally relieved that he was not going with them—and resolved not to go anywhere near the Mountain Cove Hotel, ever again.

Shane and Lucas saddled up and headed onto the road. "Where to?" Shane asked. The scholars had replenished their supplies and packed enough trail rations for them to last for a week or more, their way of thanking them for saving the hotel. That spared Shane and Lucas from foraging for what they needed, at least for a while.

Lucas shrugged. "Probably ought to end up back in Gettysburg before too long to check in and see if anyone's requested us. But after everything here, I wouldn't object to finding somewhere quiet—without vortices or elemental spirits or disappearing hotels—and taking a little time off. Read a few books. Go fishing. Play some Frisbee with the wolf. That sort of thing."

Shane grinned. "I don't think that's too much to ask. Royston gave us a bunch of new novels I'm looking forward to reading, and I'm betting we can find a nice cabin to squat in on a lake somewhere. Quentin wants to do a little deer hunting, but he says he'll share."

"And Royston did send us on our way with a nice supply of moonshine," Lucas added. "I think we're due for some R&R. Let someone else save the world for a week. We'll be back on the job soon enough."

THE END

ABOUT THE AUTHORS

Gail Z. Martin writes epic fantasy, urban fantasy, steampunk, and comedic horror for Solaris Books, Orbit Books, Falstaff Books, SOL Publishing, and Darkwind Press. Her series include Darkhurst, Assassins of Landria, Chronicles of the Necromancer, Ascendant Kingdoms Saga, Deadly Curiosities, and the Night Vigil. As Morgan Brice, she writes urban fantasy MM paranormal romance, including the Witchbane, Badlands, and Treasure Trail series.

Larry N. Martin writes and co-authors science fiction, steampunk, and urban fantasy for Solaris Books, Falstaff Books and SOL Publishing. His newest book is *The Splintered Crown,* a portal gaming fantasy. He also is the author of *Salvage Rat,* the first in a new space opera series.

Together Gail and Larry co-author the steampunk series *Iron and Blood: The Jake Desmet Adventures* and a series of related short stories: *The Storm & Fury Adventures.* Also check out the snarky monster hunter series *Spells, Salt, and Steel* set in the New Templar Knights universe, the first novella in the post-apocalyptic series Wasteland Marshals, and *Cauldron,* the first in the Joe Mack Shadow Council Files.

You can learn more about Gail and Larry at GailZMartin.com or LarryNMartin.com, join their Facebook street team The Shadow Alliance, or sign up for their newsletter at http://eepurl.com/dd5XLj.

STAY IN TOUCH

Keep up with all the newest releases and appearance news from Larry & Gail by visiting GailZMartin.com and signing up for their newsletter!

FALSTAFF BOOKS

Want to know what's new
And coming soon from
Falstaff Books?

Try This Free Ebook Sampler

https://www.instafreebie.com/free/bsZnl

Follow the link.
Download the file.
Transfer to your e-reader, phone, tablet, watch, computer, whatever.
Enjoy.